THE SHORT AND FASCINATING
TALE OF ANGELINA WHITCOMBE

Also by Sabrina Darby

On These Silken Sheets

THE SHORT AND FASCINATING TALE OF ANGELINA WHITCOMBE

SABRINA DARBY

AVONIMPULSE

An Imprint of HarperCollinsPublishers

Excerpt from *On These Silken Sheets* copyright © 2009 by Sabrina Darby.
Excerpt from *Circle of Danger* copyright © 2012 Carla Swafford.
Excerpt from *Heat Rises* copyright © 2012 Alice Brilmayer.
Excerpt from *Somebody Like You* copyright © 2012 Candis Terry.
Excerpt from *A Most Naked Solution* copyright © 2012 Anna Clevenger.

EPub Edition JULY 2012 ISBN: 9780062230713

Print Edition ISBN: 9780062230720

10 9 8 7 6 5 4 3 2 1

This one is for my mother, who kept a good portion of our romance books in the spare washer/dryer.

ACKNOWLEDGMENTS

I'd like to thank the community at The Ballroom Blog, where this novella first came alive in a series of posts. I'd also like to thank my friends and family for their support, whether it came in the form of beta reading or encouragement: my husband, sister, and parents, Sarah MacLean, Mallory Braus, Amber Anderson, and Jullie. Many thanks as well to my agent, Stephanie Cabot, and to my editor, Tessa Woodward.

The Short and Fascinating
Tale of Angelina Whitcombe

March 1816

Dear Cousin,

I still despair of ever seeing my Georgie matched.
There is one thing unchanged about my son, and that is
that nothing his mother says can make him see reason.
As a result, I've taken your advice and have placed an
advertisement in the paper. I can hear you now in my mind
claiming that you were teasing and never intended me to
realize such an action. However, I am at my wits' end and
thus have undertaken a diabolical scheme. As I am not
entirely certain my son is comfortable with ladies, I thought
perhaps to test the waters, so to speak, by finding him a
mistress.

Yours,
Mary

Chapter One

The last time Angelina Whitcombe had been this far north, it had been the end of summer, when the loveliness of the rolling, green earth of the Dales was at its finest and the river sparkled in the sunlight.

Instead, it was spring and snow still clung stubbornly to shady corners and mist lingered over the faded road dotted with rocks and fallen trees. Thankfully, she'd prepared for every eventuality of weather. After all, everything she owned was packed into the trunk, back at the inn. It had been a bit of a shock to see twenty-two years of life fold down into a space four feet by two feet.

Through the canopy of branches she glimpsed a sight of gray. *The tower. Finally.*

And it wasn't all that far away.

She picked her way around yet another large fallen tree branch. The winds had ravaged the area and no one cared enough about this overgrown road to clear it. But once upon a time, people must have traversed it daily, otherwise no one would have thought this area important enough to build a castle.

To build the now ruined tower house in which Mrs. Martin claimed her scarred and diffident war hero son had hidden himself away. It seemed fitting enough for a gothic novel: ruined castle, ruined man.

With a slight twist, for Angelina's employment was to seduce the poor invalid, reawaken in him a sense of the erotic, and then encourage him to seek a wife. She had little doubt she could do the first. After all, she was no simpering virgin. She'd been the mistress to two well-pleased men. Beyond that, she was an actress born and bred, spawned from a family of actors.

But as for the last . . . well, she'd find a way to fulfill her duty in some fashion. Regardless, she'd walk away from this transaction a hundred pounds richer. Once she would have scoffed at that sum of money, but not now. Her value in London had plummeted and a hundred pounds could keep a wise woman for years.

She stopped, took a deep calming breath. There was no point in anger or resentment. She had to focus on the task at hand, which required being charming and frothy, lifting a man out of the depths of despair.

She shifted the leather-bound sketchbook she carried from her left arm to her right, rolled her shoulders back in a stretch and then started forward again. If this traipsing about country lanes was to become a habit, she would need sturdier shoes.

The lane turned to the left, the trees opening into a clearing, and there the castle was before her on a slight rise. She frowned.

It wasn't a very large castle. In fact, it was neither pictur-esquely ruined nor perfectly upkept. It looked . . . disheveled more than anything.

Fitting. She could feel wisps of her hair against her cheeks and neck. Likely she, too, looked a bit disheveled. Preferably, she looked windblown and rosy-cheeked, the very picture of bucolic English femininity.

She stopped again halfway up the glacis, catching her breath. When she'd been a young girl, she'd run across hill and dale, skipped across meadows and scampered along rivers. Now, she was already tired from the long walk from the village and this small elevation was taxing her greatly.

As she took several deep breaths, she studied the tower. The thick, wooden door was ajar. Excellent. It would be much easier to saunter in as if she thought the place abandoned than to knock and beg entrance.

She trudged uphill. As she neared the door, a clanging filled the air and the earth seemed to shake. She stopped again and listened carefully, trying to identify the discordant sounds. Mrs. Martin had assured her that Captain H. J. G. Martin, or *"my poor Georgie,"* was the only occupant of the castle, but what if he was not here? What if ruffians or high-waymen had taken up residence? What if she was about to put herself in a situation far worse and more dangerous than the one she had fled from in London?

She looked around. She could flee now, head back to the village. Although really, having come all this way, it was a bit late for those sorts of thoughts.

Forward again.

The clanging had more of a rhythm now—sounded like

metal against wood. Maybe this Captain Martin was not alone, and had hired a carpenter or some other craftsmen to bring the place to rights.

She slipped through the doorway. Hesitantly, she walked across the dim antechamber and entered a large room. The great hall, she imagined it would have been called. Here, light streamed in through windows high off the ground, and straight ahead, flames simmered in the large fireplace.

The clanging continued, but there was no one in this sparsely furnished room.

"Hello?" she called out. She slowly crossed the hall, running her hand over the lone table covered with rolls of paper that stood in the middle of the room, pausing by neatly folded blankets and a pallet of straw by the fire. She eyed the large wooden tub tucked to the right of the big stone hearth.

Someone lived here. *Slept* here.

Captain Martin or a squatter?

The conditions were worse than the ones she had grown up in as a child in an impoverished traveling theater troupe.

"Is there someone here?" she said, projecting her voice as loudly as she could. It echoed off stone walls. The clanging hesitated, continued for a moment and then, finally, stopped. She was scared to leave this spacious, empty room to venture into more shadowy spaces beyond the archway to her left.

Instead, she focused on the stack of books beside the makeshift bed. Curious, she knelt down, feeling the warmth from the fire on her face as she reached for the one on top.

She heard the panting a moment before a large furry animal charged at her.

She swiveled her head, lost her balance, and slipped back

onto the floor, her sketchbook falling to the side. The dog, a collie, pressed its large wet nose against the side of her face.

"Jasper, heel. Who the devil are you?"

Wonderful. Likely the dog's owner was Captain Martin and there would be no graceful way to rise from such an indelicate position on her own.

She looked up, raised her hand for assistance and then dropped her hand.

Dropped her jaw, too, before she caught herself.

He was bare to the chest and magnificent. Strong, with muscles as defined as if a sculptor had chiseled them from marble, skin glistening from whatever physical effort in which he had been engaged. The clothed parts of him were wonderful too. Her gaze slid down the lines of his hips and thighs, before the place where the superfluous fabric of the trousers obscured what were surely equally fine calves. How could they not be? This man in front of her was some god of male perfection.

"Madam." There was a hardened edge to that voice, and reluctantly, Angelina lifted her gaze to meet his. Which was obdurate, and yet he smirked at her. As if he were both angry and amused.

"I'm very sorry to disturb you," she said at last, lifting her hand toward him for assistance once more. She punctuated her words with the smile that had charmed audiences across England. "I'd been told there was a ruined castle to see. I thought it abandoned until I heard that fracas. Help me up, will you?"

He stepped forward out of the shadows and she gasped at the sight of the jagged scar that cut from cheek to chin, twisting his lips up on one side. There wasn't anything amused about this man looming over her. Now she'd made the situation worse by staring.

At least that shocking feature confirmed without a doubt that this man, who looked the antithesis of shy and sickly, was the very man she intended to seduce. The way he fairly radiated masculinity, this wouldn't be hard at all. In fact, it would be her *pleasure*.

"This is a private residence," he said, even as he reached his hand out. His large, strong, bare hand that made her wish she wasn't wearing gloves. She placed her fingers on his palm and used her ballet training to rise to her feet as gracefully as possible.

He had a very warm hand.

When she was standing, looking up into that scowling, smirking face, she didn't let go.

"Yes," she purred. "I see. Do you live here . . . alone?"

He snatched his hand away, stepping back. Looked pointedly toward the front door.

Of course, she couldn't leave. And now that she'd seen him, she didn't really want to. What she wanted to do was run her hands over his naked skin, lick the small nipples that dotted the fine smattering of hair down his chest. While sexual relations had mostly been an economic transaction for her, while this, at the heart of it all, would be too, she rather thought she'd want to taste this man even if she weren't being paid.

Which was stupid. Was the way women like her went from being beloved mistresses of marquesses and earls to roadside whores.

No. She had a job to do.

"I'm in Yorkshire to draw the Dales," she said into the charged silence. "I've stopped at the Golden Lion in the village and they assured me Castle Auldale is as ruined and picturesque as old abandoned castles come. 'Tis a pity I only draw landscapes. You are equally picturesque."

His eyebrows rose and he crossed his arms, but still he didn't speak. Just watched her with that expression, which was confused by the perpetual twist of his lips.

"What? Surely you have women fainting in your path wherever you go? You cannot be ignorant of your physical appeal?"

His arms fell back to his sides. He looked deliciously nonplussed. Which meant she had the upper hand. Which meant––he was just where she needed him. Intrigued.

"Who are you?" he said, the words hissing through the air.

"Angelina Whitcombe, and as I said, I'm traveling for the scenery."

"Traveling alone?"

A prickle of awareness awakened the skin at the back of her neck.

"Yes, in fact, I am."

His gaze ran down her body, slowly, purposefully, as if he wanted to make certain that she knew exactly what he was looking at.

"A lady never travels alone."

The best lies were half-truths, so she smiled brilliantly at him.

"Darling, I don't have much of a reputation left to lose."

"*I don't have much of a reputation left to lose.*"

He believed her. He just didn't believe that devil-may-care, forward I. No, there was the hint of something much deeper, and much darker, beneath his intruder's flippant words.

Not that it mattered.

He wanted this Whitcombe woman out of his home, away from the solitude he'd so carefully cultivated. If he wanted human company, he would be living in the manor house half a mile across the dale.

"But I do," he said at last, reaching down to pick up her leather-bound sketchbook. "So I must ask you to leave." He held the book out to her, tempted to open it and see just what she had been sketching during her *tour* of the English countryside. She snatched it away.

"I suppose I should be getting back before it grows dark. I embarked on my walk rather late in the day." But instead of leaving, she swept past him toward the archway that led farther into the keep. "What *are* you doing in here?"

He strode after her, shaking his head. He grabbed her by the elbow before she could leave the room.

She stepped back as if he'd pulled on her harder than he had, and all of a sudden an armful of soft, warm woman pressed against him, blond hair tickling his nose.

He took a deep breath, which was a mistake as the scent of muguet and spring air infiltrated him, clouded his thoughts.

"You have the advantage of me, sir," she whispered, her voice low, seductive. "If we are to touch so intimately, at least I should know your name."

"John," he choked out, releasing her as if she were a flame. He did *not* wish to be intimate.

"John," she repeated. She made his name sound like a word lovers whispered in the dark of night. She turned to face him. "What secrets are you hiding?"

Secrets? He had no secrets. Everything about his life could be found in the local church records, in the army register, in the files of the Board of Ordnance.

He didn't know who this woman was, but he knew she was dangerous. He knew she was taking him away from the work he wanted to do, the work that was helping him, saving him. She was the outside world seeping in.

"Out," he demanded. "Now."

He must have looked frightening. God knew he had scared enough children with this scarred countenance of his. She, too, had gasped when she'd first seen him. Now she winced and retreated.

Good. She should think him dangerous. What woman in her right mind would stand in the middle of a ruined castle talking to a half-clothed stranger? He was a man, stronger than her. He could rape her, kill her. No one would ever know.

He closed his eyes tight against memories. Against the deafening sound of metal striking metal, wordless battle cries, and explosions. Against the smell of blood and gunpowder.

She was walking away, the soft soles of her shoes tapping against the stone floor. He felt her passage like a sweet, spring breeze, the scent of lilies cutting through his mind.

He opened his eyes. Through the speckled, gauzy mid-afternoon light streaming from the high windows, he caught the last flutter of her blue cloak as she turned the corner, the ribbons of her bonnet in her right hand streaming behind.

Jasper whined.

John looked down. The dog kicked its legs in the air, begging for attention.

"All right, Jasper," he said, bending down to pat the dog's flank firmly, "that was unexpected, but it doesn't change anything. We have work to do and only a few hours of daylight left."

At the moment, "work" was repairing the kitchens.

CHAPTER TWO

When he went out the following day to draw water from the nearby beck, the woman had returned, this time sitting on a blanket she'd spread at the base of the grassy slope, which was surely cold and damp. She was bent industriously over her sketchbook, and when she looked up again, she smiled widely and raised a hand in greeting. Jasper was already bounding over to her, curious as always.

He could ignore her. Or he could find out why she was here, where she clearly wasn't wanted.

She closed her sketchbook, suffered Jasper's attentions even as she ran her hands through his fur.

Life was much easier as a dog.

Stoically, John approached her.

"No plumbing? Or at least a well?" she asked. Her arms were full with a very happy collie, but she gestured with her chin to the two empty buckets John carried.

"The well requires considerable attention to be of any use, and the plumbing is rudimentary. Water would have been kept at a cistern on the roof of the tower and pumped down

as needed. There is neither roof nor cistern at the moment."
His mouth felt as dry as the words. He hadn't been asked to
give a lecture on the workings of castles and fortifications.

Yet she looked fascinated.

"You are trying to restore the castle to habitation?" she
asked. Jasper broke away and took off down the hill in pursuit
of a bird.

How to answer that?

"I gathered from the noise yesterday," she continued,
pushing herself up to her feet. "The great hall seemed remarkably preserved, but——" She gestured to the castle behind him,
which he knew bore the mark of battle and abandonment.
The curtain wall and outbuildings had already been reduced
to foundations to provide stone for other works in the area,
including the manor house. "Why are you doing this on your
own? Surely one man alone cannot restore all of this?"

"I don't know," he answered at last. "It could be done. I've
drawn the plans." He saw the carefully rendered designs in
his mind, the survey he'd taken, possible modification. "It
would take many skilled artificers, laborers. No, I could not
do it alone. But I want to."

Because he needed to be grounded by the feel of stone
under his hands, of iron, wood, earth. He needed to lose himself in something that required all his thought and attention.

Because he was trying to forget.

He clenched his hands. His empty hands. At some point,
without realizing, he'd placed the buckets down. A silent surrender to her presence.

To the way the wind was pushing at the brim of her
bonnet, flicking about the loose tendrils of hair at her tem-

ples. She had blue eyes. Pale, clear eyes rimmed by an almost greenish ring.

He picked up the buckets and walked away. Focused on the way the earth felt beneath his boots as he strode toward the beck, flattening grass as he went.

"Did I upset you?"

She was following him, but he didn't stop. There was work to be done. He would just have to pretend she wasn't there. That he wasn't curious. That he didn't wonder why she'd returned after he'd made it quite clear she wasn't welcome.

"Captain Martin!"

He stopped and turned. She stopped abruptly too, less than an arm's length from him, and looked up, breathless. Her chest rose and fell rapidly under her voluminous winter clothes as she caught her breath.

"I gathered your identity from the villagers. You walk fast."

"Why are you here?"

She was looking at him carefully, the intensity of her study making him tense in awareness.

He acknowledged the attraction. She was both lovely and odd. A puzzle, and he had always enjoyed puzzles.

Only now, he preferred them inanimate, uncomplicated by the uglier side of human interactions. Of the animal instinct that made men act dishonorably.

"I told you . . ." She fell quiet. It was that silence he listened to, the inner workings of her thoughts as they shifted, as she decided what she would tell him. She sighed and then offered him the barest hint of a smile. "It's rather cold out here." She gestured to his chest, made him aware that he was covered only by the thin barrier of a shirt. "Why don't you fetch that water and I'll meet you inside? Over a cup of tea, I'll tell you the short and *fascinating* tale of Angelina Whitcombe."

The story of why she had no reputation.

He wanted to know. But he wanted to know on a piece of paper, distanced, as if it really were some morality play.

A flicker of something dark passed across her face. All at once he felt the chill of the day. He'd been still too long.

"Miss Whitcombe." She didn't correct his address and so he continued. "Do you do this frequently? Stalk men? Invade their homes.

"Not quite."

He laughed, despite himself. What an answer!

"I should read the papers more regularly. I'm certain there is a warning: damnable female, invading homes and pestering them with promises of her peculiar tale."

She smiled, but it was a thin curve of the lips. Hollow.

"I'll meet you inside, Captain."

He watched her go without argument, watched her cross the open land back to where she'd left her blanket and book. She knelt down to fold the cloth.

She was a strange and lovely vision on an unseasonably cold spring day. Her blue coat was bright against the grass, falling in picturesque folds.

Picturesque. She'd called him that only yesterday.

Shaking his head, he turned toward the water again and whistled for Jasper.

The inside of the great hall looked very much the way it had the day before. The air was thick with dust that sparkled in the filtered light. One wooden bench stood by the large, cluttered table. Other than that, the only other seating was the stone window seats. Which was just as well for her purposes.

She stopped by the fire and took off her outer layers: gloves, coat, bonnet. Then she inspected his makeshift bed before settling herself down on it.

He was intrigued, his interest obvious, but he fought against the attraction. Yet events were moving fast, considering she'd only known him a matter of minutes, less than an hour really.

At this rate she could have him bedded by sundown. A few days of erotic attention and she could collect her earnings. This entire episode would be merely a small sliver in her memory, completely forgettable if not for the fact that the good Captain was enormously attractive, even with that hideous scar.

There was no point in lingering and spending more time when the fee was set. Instead, she'd move on, perhaps to York or Edinburgh, somewhere she could settle herself, find work in a theater or with a new protector. Somewhere, hopefully, gossip would not have reached.

She could change her name, too.

His footsteps sounded by the door, which he closed behind him against the wind. Jasper caught sight of her, and then bounded across the room, as if he hadn't seen her just minutes ago.

The captain came more slowly. Pushing Jasper's enthusiastic head away from her face, she watched his master walk across the room, enjoyed the sight of his long, muscled body engaged in action, arms flexed with the weight of the full buckets of water.

Servant work. Or soldier work, she supposed.

He set the buckets down, against the wall. Studied her with that eternally amused expression. She shifted her attention to his eyes, which she knew now to be brown—a very solid, warm brown—but looked darker in the shadows of the hall.

What was he thinking? Feeling?

She shifted over a bit and patted next to her on the pallet.

He snapped his fingers and Jasper scrambled from her side to lie down a few feet away, the dog's head perked up watchfully.

"The best salons in London could learn from your design choices," she said lightly. "Surprisingly comfortable, if scratchy."

"I've slept on worse." His words were thick, sparse, but he came closer, sat down beside her.

A small thrill of excitement filled her as she watched him fold himself down to the floor, legs outstretched. He was so big, and so close. So raw.

"I'm certain you have, Captain," she said. "But you've done your duty, I'm sure. Risked your life for our country." Risked his face as well, she thought, her fingers itching to touch him, to run over that scar, but it was too soon. She needed to let the intimacy build, the tension in the narrow space between them rise. "Would it not be easier to spend your nights at the manor and come here only during the day?"

"No."

He didn't elaborate. Instead he lay down on his side, propping his head up on his arm. With his right hand he plucked at a piece of straw that peeked out from under the blankets. He looked idle, relaxed, as if they were friends or lovers.

She relaxed a fraction more as well.

Then he focused the entirety of his attention on her. Her skin prickled with awareness. The false, forced intimacy doing its magic on her as well. Which was good. The best performances always built on a kernel of truth.

"You have a story for me, Miss Whitcombe."

"Angelina."

He raised an eyebrow but said nothing. She looked down and away, pressing her lips tight against an errant, embarrassed smile.

"Yes, I did promise you one, Captain." She said the words slowly, formulating her strategy. Did she seduce him now, before admitting she was a professional at love, or did she tell him her story, set any moral reservations at rest with the knowledge?

"John," he corrected. She met his gaze again.

"You said as much yesterday, but they called you Captain George Martin in the village."

His lips, so twisted already, tightened. "I prefer John."

"Well, then, John," she said with a bright smile, "the last time I slept on a bed like this, I was seventeen and with my parents, who traveled with a theater troupe. My father is an actor, my mother made costumes. I'd been taking on bit parts, had done a turn as Helena in *A Midsummer's Night's Dream*. That was the summer I allowed myself to be seduced by a very handsome new actor. He told me I could do better than a makeshift stage at village markets. I followed him to London. And he was right."

"So you're an actress."

There was a note of understanding to his statement, and she smiled ruefully. Her own choices had underscored the salacious reputation actresses received.

"I was very good on the boards . . . and in the beds."

CHAPTER THREE

She was in *his* bed, even if it was a poor excuse for one. She sat with her legs tucked under her, and the fabric of her dress accentuated the curve of her hip, the long lengths of her thighs. The swell of her breasts. If he shifted slightly, he could lay his head in her lap, rest there surrounded by her voluptuousness.

He looked back down at the much-worried length of straw in his hand.

Regardless of her profession, of the strangeness of this encounter, she didn't deserve to be molested by his thoughts.

A blur of movement alerted him the instant before her gentle fingers touched his face, the unscarred cheek, and his gaze flew back to hers. There was no mistaking the seductive invitation in her eyes, in the small smile that played at the corners of her lips. It was as if she had read his mind.

The space between them nearly crackled with energy.

He sat up quickly, pushing himself away from her so that he leaned against the stone wall.

Her hand fell back into her lap, but she still looked at him, heating him up with her eyes.

"Yesterday," she continued softly, leaning closer. He found himself inching toward her, too, bending his head slightly to hear her words, to let his left ear, the one whose function was not as damaged by the volume of war, catch every sound. "I wanted to draw the castle, but today . . ." She paused, looking him straight in the eyes with those pale ones, and fascinated, he waited for her to finish. " . . . Today, I just want you."

His breath released in a stunned exhale.

Bold. Plainspoken. No wonder she had no reputation of which to speak. Or maybe she'd never had a reputation, born as she had been into a profession that leant itself to disrepute.

He was aroused, heat settling heavily in his groin. He enjoyed the sensation. It was rare these days that he thought of sexual pleasure.

Why shouldn't he accept this woman's unvarnished invitation? It had been long enough since he'd engaged in intimate relations. This would be consensual.

But that thought alone, suggesting the other, the nonconsensual, was cold water over his growing interest.

"I'm not in the market for a mistress." He pressed against the stone as if it could ground him, could make sense of the swirling heat in his skin.

"And I'm not in the market to be your mistress," she shot back. She looked offended and he wondered how he could have so misread everything. "You're nothing like the men I want: titled, exceedingly wealthy. You live in a crumbling castle, and sleep on a straw pallet."

"This castle is a ruin on my estate, which includes the manor house down the road."

"Are you trying to entice me to seduce you?"

He laughed, shocked. She laughed too. A low, husky sound, suggestive and knowing.

"I do mean what I say, John. I have no wish to be kept by you. But . . . that doesn't mean we can't enjoy ourselves during my brief sojourn in Auldale."

He wanted to bury his face in his hands, hide from the temptation. He reached for words desperately.

"Why Auldale?"

She stared at him. Challenging him.

"John?" she pressed.

"Why?" he managed to ask. But he finished the question silently. *Why did you come here to disturb my peace? Why make me want you when I'm not ready to feel this desire again?*

"I lived not so far from here, briefly, in my youth, and I was happy here."

He relaxed fractionally, relieved she had chosen to interpret his question as a continuation of the previous.

"And what made you leave London?"

Any of the men she'd known in London would have had her skirts up to her waist by then. Mrs. Martin had sought professional help for her son, and clearly, there was a reason why. But John's impressive physique had somewhat blinded Angelina to the truth. There was something wrong with him that went deeper that the scar that twisted his mouth.

Or he simply wasn't attracted to her.

But from the way he looked at her, the way he reacted to the smallest touch, she rather thought he did want her.

So why not simply take what was offered?

Unless he knew he couldn't. She'd heard of such an ailment, particularly in syphilitic men, but she didn't think that disease was the problem here. Perhaps he had other war injuries that lay beneath his trousers. What a shame.

But how could she determine such a thing? It was one thing to proposition the man the day after first meeting him. It was another entirely to ask him about his ability to achieve an erection.

She'd simply have to . . . create the situation in which she could entice him and then feel the physical evidence of his desire. Subtlety would be necessary, which required more time.

But he was still waiting for her answer. Why had she left London?

"Because my last patron's new mistress decided London wasn't big enough for the two of us." She ran her finger over the edge of a fold of the blanket beneath her, and then looked over her shoulder into the flames of the fire. With effort, she unclenched her jaw and relaxed her face into a more attractive profile. She might still be angry over the situation, but much of the reason she'd had to leave London was her own stupidity. She hadn't saved for the future, planned for a day she was not courted and feted or desired by wealthy men.

Not that she couldn't find another protector, but it was much easier when one was on the stage, nearly naked and posturing in front of their eyes.

"She had me dismissed from the theater where we both performed. But that wasn't enough. She ensured that *no one* in London would hire me this spring."

"Jealousy or revenge?"

Nearly an offhand question but he had cut to the quick of it all.

"Both," she admitted. "As I had numerous creditors and no income, I sold what I could and chose a well-timed retreat."

She tossed her head with a sigh, willing all the troubling thoughts away. All that mattered was being here, now, in this strange castle in the middle of the wilds with a handsome, injured man who she was contracted to seduce.

He nodded.

The flames were low, and a draft sent a shiver through her. She drew her knees up, wrapped her arms around them and then rested her chin. She stared at him, waiting for him to say something.

Anything.

But he seemed far away, deep in thought.

"I . . ." he said finally, and the brief utterance sounded thick. "This castle is *my* retreat."

He met her gaze, his brown eyes so deep, so sentient. The draft rushed over her again, raising the hair on her arms, the back of her neck.

"Would you show it to me?" she said abruptly, shifting again to tuck her legs under her. "I know you have work to do and I've taken so much of your time as it is, but I'd love to see. I'd love to know your plans for it."

"Yes, of course," he said, his tone light as well, as if he too wished to dispel the darkness with its deep shadows. He pushed himself away from the wall and stood, holding his hand out to help her.

Angelina rested her fingers on his palm, and this time was different from the day before: his rough, work-textured skin teased at the sensitive ends of her bare fingers. She let go of his hand as soon as she was steady on her feet. This was a truce of sorts.

He gestured to the long length of the nearly empty great hall. "This was not part of the original keep. In fact, Castle Auldale is quite unusual in its construction. It started as a simple tower: the kitchens and storage rooms were the ground floor, then above was the main hall and above that a solar. There is a narrow spiral staircase that provides access." His voice had changed during the recitation. Whatever dark emotion had prompted him to share that brief intimacy earlier had transformed into a scientific enthusiasm. "Come." He swiveled on his heel and strode toward the archway that had framed her first sight of him. Jasper sprung to his feet and trotted behind his master. Angelina followed too.

The space was darker, damper, instantly several degrees cooler, and the air was thick with the dust of construction. In the light that shimmered down from above, she could see planks of wood piled against the wall, waiting for whatever he intended to do.

"This was the kitchen in the original keep," he continued. "Beyond that door is a storage room, also original."

"That door surely isn't original," she observed. The wood construction looked simple, new. The iron of its handle modern.

"Correct. That was one of my first improvements. Anything made of the original timber has long since rotted away. The reason the beams of the great hall still exist is that the hall is of more recent provenance. In fact, look up."

She looked up. Glimpsed a fragment of cloudy Yorkshire sky high above.

"These stone vaults suspended the first floor. You can see that most of the remaining wood is rotted. I cut through the worst of it to allow light in. For now.

"The vaults are not original either. They were likely added nearly a century after the original keep."

She stared at the ruins around her, at the places where stone had fallen away or wood looked charred from excessive exposure to the rain. She knew that many of the country's homes were several centuries old, had been improved upon and changed with each generation. Even the theaters had their tumultuous histories. But she'd never seen the passage of time exposed this way.

"That would have been, what, the fourteenth century?"

"Yes, approximately. My great-grandfather came into possession of the castle and lands in 1742. There are, unfortunately, very few records existent."

He claimed ownership so casually, naturally, and yet without any of the sense of entitlement her previous, titled lovers had displayed. What made John Martin tick? Seduction aside, she wanted to peel back his layers as thoroughly as he had those of the castle. She wanted to *know* him. Naturally, it was of the utmost importance to study the habits of one's quarry.

He showed her the rest of the castle interior, stopping her from climbing the stairs, which were worn down by time, chipped by war and slickened by moss. He showed her his plans for modernization and expansion, to take something that had been left to crumble and rot, which had been destroyed to create other buildings, and turn it into an interesting and comfortable retreat. Then they walked about the exterior, and he pointed out the remnants of the curtain wall and of the outbuildings.

The afternoon sun had broken through the heavy layer of clouds and now glinted off Angelina's hair, illuminated her pale skin. He could very well imagine her on a stage, commanding the audience's attention. She was rounded and yet lithe, had a presence that made her seem tall, but she was half a head shorter than him. She possessed sophisticated London airs and yet she was following him about, asking questions as if she were absolutely fascinated by architecture and medieval fortifications.

The basest, most male part of him was responding to that attention, pleased at her interest, at the way those pale eyes looked up at him admiringly.

"I've taken up half your afternoon, Captain Martin," she said. He looked at the slant of the shadows, which had grown longer. Barely an hour left before dark. Evening really, but she was likely still on London time, where the sunset was merely the start to the day's activities. "It's been a great pleasure and I thank you."

Common courtesies stilled on his tongue. She had invaded his peace. Was he really to thank her for that?

He nodded finally, and stood aside, his chest tight.

"Well, then." She seemed to realize he planned to say nothing and turned away from him, toward the main door of the keep, the very opposite direction of the village. She was certainly persistent. He rubbed at his cheek, at the still uncomfortable twinge of skin and muscle pulling against the scar.

But inside, she confounded him once again, stopping only to gather her belongings. There was no overt seduction or excuse to stay longer. He watched her take her leave with the sense that he was losing something.

Something ineffable, like camaraderie or companionship, pleasures he forwent because there were no humans on earth with whom he wished to converse beyond a scientific exchange through letters and books, or a basic and quickly passed mercantile exchange.

He preferred this world he had created, the one that encompassed only he and Jasper, who whined now by the door, which had closed behind Angelina.

Everything was going quite well. Back at the inn, she had finally been able to slip out of her increasingly uncomfortable shoes and order a hot meal from the innkeeper. Now, as the sun was setting, she rested on the rather comfortable bed—the inn was really quite clean and neat as inns went—with her feet up and her copy of *A Midsummer Night's Dream* at her side. She may as well put these interminable evenings and nights to good use. She had not expected to have her hours so empty of activity and the previous night she had finished the one novel she had brought with her. Perhaps there was a local circulating library. Or some other traveler in the inn would take pity on her and engage in a round of chess. Not that she thought there were any other travelers at the inn. Perhaps later in the week, closer to market day, there would be increased activity.

But there were no theaters or pleasure gardens, masquerades or soirees. There was nowhere a lady of her position could go. Not that anyone but John knew she was a courtesan, but she was traveling alone, which was odd enough. She could hardly present herself at the manor house and demand Mrs. Martin provide entertainment.

In any event, she was getting older, and soon she'd not be fit for Helena or Hermia, so she intended to brush up on Titania's lines. It would be amusing to play the Queen of the Fairies.

She would be on the stage again. Perhaps in York or some other large town at first, but eventually, she could return to London. Elizabeth Duncan's time as celebrated actress would not last long. She was a talentless novelty.

Angelina closed her eyes, taking deep even breaths. Anger would achieve nothing other than to age her faster. Much better to think about something under her immediate control. Or someone.

Like Captain Martin.

John.

He had strong, lean arms, and against the rolled-up cuffs of his white sleeves, she'd admired the tanned cast of his skin, the fine hair that tapered down toward his wrist. She had a weakness for a man's forearms, for wrists and hands, and John was well-endowed in that area.

There was always that old wives' tale about hands. Not that Angelina had found that true in her limited experience. Lord Alverley had possessed lovely hands but was quite diminished in other charms. Fortunately, he had also been possessed with a fortune and a kind, generous nature. She'd been his mistress for two years after reaching London. If he hadn't chosen to be faithful upon marriage, she'd likely be his mistress still.

She'd really been quite fortunate in her lovers. Gentlemen all. If only Lord Peter Denham had been possessed of a more independent mind and not swayed to betray Angelina by that horrible Lizzie.

There she was again, thinking about the past.

She could not change it. She could only bide her time and plan.

And seduce John, who desired her but did not want to be seduced.

Yesterday, she had returned to the inn convinced that he did indeed wish to be left alone, but tonight . . . tonight it seemed very clear that his mother was correct; he needed to be drawn out. He wanted to be drawn out.

She imagined what the expression on his face would be when the following day he found her attempting an artistic rendition of his ruined castle yet again.

CHAPTER FOUR

John woke with the sun. He stretched his arms and then propped his head on his hands and stared up at the thick wooden beams that crossed the ceiling. Next to him, Jasper was a warm pressure against his thigh. He liked waking here, with the last embers of the previous night's fire still glowing red, as if he lived in a world apart, hidden.

But something was different this morning.

The castle had always held an open, unformed sense of possibility. It had been untouched by humans for at least a century; though he knew visitors had come, none had attempted to since he resided there. News traveled fast in small towns.

Yet Angelina had come, and now he could still feel her presence here before the hearth, vibrating through him as solidly as Jasper's snores.

Disturbing.

At least that sensation would dissipate quickly. The odd episode had passed and he could continue on as before. He pushed the blankets off and stood. Jasper made a plaintive noise and John glanced back down to find the collie staring at him, kicking his legs, tangling the covers more.

He laughed and squatted down to run his hands briskly through Jasper's fur. Then with two firm pats to the dog's flank, he stopped and stood again. There was much to do today if he intended to have the castle fully habitable by next winter.

He went about his morning ablutions, went down to the stream for more water, and then prepared his morning toast from one of the loaves of bread he took from the manor every Sunday. Then he unrolled the newest of his plans for the tower and studied them as he ate.

It was a far cry from the first day he had explored the castle. He hadn't been to the ruins since before entering Woolwich Academy as a cadet, but instantly he'd visualized the renovation project. He'd ordered all the newest literature on construction methods and innovations, and then had started working on his plans. In the five months that he'd been working on the castle, he'd made considerable progress. He'd started with simple things: cleaning the rubble out from the interior, ensuring the fireplace was in working order, fixing the holes in the roof of the great hall. Once he'd made himself a livable space, he'd moved out of the manor house and then progress had grown exponentially. He'd painstakingly dug down into the dirt floors of what had once been the kitchen and beneath the thick exterior walls to lay pipes for drainage. Now he was working on reconstructing the wood planks of the first floor.

Armed with axe and saw, John ventured out of the castle just past noon to chop more wood for scaffolding. She was there again, the ribbons of her bonnet streaming behind her in the light breeze as she attempted to lay down a blanket on the grass. The same wind that so charmingly pressed her skirts against her legs, twisted the blanket, until finally, Angelina caught sight of him, stopped fighting the wind, and waved.

He had underestimated her determination to draw the castle.

Or to have an affair.

Heat rushed through him. He'd had his youthful infatuations and the usual affairs. Once, he wouldn't have questioned a woman's interest. But now . . . he forced himself to look away, go about his work.

It was a beautiful spring day.

After John disappeared around the bend, Angelina returned to her attempts to lay the blanket smoothly on the ground. Finally, she gave up and sat down, smoothing it out around her once she was settled. But the wind was strong and even in all of her layers of clothing, she couldn't muster up any enthusiasm for art under these blustery conditions. She had hoped to bide her time this morning, let the idea of her outside, drawing, grow in his mind until he wanted her to come in and keep him company.

She needed a new plan. One that involved sitting inside, preferably near the fire. Perhaps she could work on a still life, or a study of his dog.

She stood up again, gathered her belongings, and relocated.

Inside.

Wouldn't he be surprised?

Jasper met her halfway across the great hall, sniffing about her, sticking his nose up against the large wicker basket she carried. She'd come prepared.

She decided to settle herself in the middle of the stone floor and spread her blanket there. The fire and pallet would make an unusual subject for art. Later, though. She opened the basket and cut a slice of sausage for the dog before carefully selecting her own food. The innkeeper had prepared a fine cold repast.

Jasper stayed close, making low, plaintive growling sounds in his throat. By the time John finally returned, she'd fed the dog two sausages, which Jasper had eaten as if he'd never had anything as delicious before in his life.

"There you are." John loomed over her, backlit by the midday sun that filtered in, his features indefinable. Even two feet from her, she felt heat radiating off his body. No wonder he could go about in just his shirtsleeves.

"Were you worried I'd left?" she teased.

"Terrified."

"It was cold outside, so I thought I'd picnic in here. You should join me. I had the innkeeper pack for two." She looked sidelong at Jasper, who was watching every move she made. "There's even enough for three."

John laughed. "I can hardly refuse an invitation like that. I'll be back in a moment."

She watched him walk over to the hearth. He had a long, purposeful stride, and as he walked, the fabric of his trousers molded to different parts of his well-shaped body. He washed his face and hands in one of the two buckets. If only he would take off that shirt again. Let water pour down those muscles.

Angelina looked away quickly, a bit shocked at the direction of her thoughts. She wasn't missish; she was experienced, for goodness sake. But this was a pure lust like she'd never felt before.

Her cheeks were still hot when he sat down next to her, stretching his legs out and leaning over to look inside the open basket.

Like dog, like master.

She pulled out the carefully wrapped packages: thickly sliced ham, pickles, cheese and bread. There were buns and tarts, and a jug of ale as well. Men rarely ate the noontime meal, and as he must be fending for himself, she doubted that, if he did eat at this hour, it was anything as indulgent.

He helped himself to a generous portion, stacking food on bread in a thick sandwich. If the way to a man's heart was through his stomach, she was well on that path.

"How long do you intend to stay in Auldale?" he asked between bites.

"I'm not entirely certain. Until I grow weary of it, I suppose," she met his eyes for an instant before he looked back into the basket. "Or until I wear out my welcome."

"Ah." He was busy eating, as if, as he finished the sandwich and reached for more food, he were barely attending what she was saying, but she had the sense he heard everything, that he had thoughts, opinions.

When would he voice them?

Would he voice them?

"At some point," she continued, to break up the growing silence, "I'll return to the theater. I'll return to London."

He put down a drumstick, licked his fingers. "For now, you want to hide, lick your wounds. Gain strength."

Her breath caught.

The air felt a little thick, the air a bit too dusty and stinging her eyes.

"I wouldn't want to stop you from finishing your drawings of the castle. Someone should draw it for posterity, after all."

The invitation was clear and her chest ached a bit. He thought her wounded, in need of a rescuer. The lovely man was playing his own, taciturn, version of a knight on a white horse.

Which was romantic and sweet.

While she was there under false pretenses.

She wasn't speaking. Perhaps he'd been too blunt. Perhaps she preferred to pretend she had everything under control, that she wasn't devastated at having to leave her life in London. That a strange sojourn in the north of Yorkshire in one of the coldest years in recent history was exactly how she had intended to spend the height of the London season.

Certainly, why should she admit her fears to him? A certain kinship might be there, but they were strangers.

He needed to lighten the mood.

"Nor would I stop you from picnicking on the ground."

She laughed. There, that was better. He liked the sound of her laughter. It was rich and warm and made him want to taste it. Taste her.

Not that he would take advantage of her, despite her

sexual invitation of the day before. She expected men to desire her, to use desire and coitus as currency.

"So easily, you could have all the comforts you wish," she teased, shifting her weight, moving her feet to her other side. He caught a glimpse of stocking-clad calves above her half boots. Shapely calves. Bare, they would be even shapelier. "I'm certain that at the manor, meals aren't served on a blanket over hard stone."

It was a ridiculous image, this strange picnic transposed to the inside the dining room of the manor house. But there, the blanket would be a thick woolen rug over the polished wood floor, and Angelina's blond hair would be perfectly framed by the rich fabrics and textures.

"If they were, perhaps I'd have stayed."

"Truly though, what of the rest of your estate? I thought landowners had duties . . ."

Duties. Like continuing to fight for one's country even after one had lost faith.

He studiously picked an apple out of the basket and bit into it. His loud crunching punctuated the silence.

During the first days home he had sat down at the large oak desk that had once been his father's, consulted with his mother, the steward and tenants. Pored over ledgers and accounts. Exchanged letters with their banker in York.

"It was kept well in my absence," he said finally. "There is little that requires my attention. Some men hunt, or ride, or spend their days in study of natural history. This"—he gestured to the room around them—"is how I choose to spend my time."

He wiped his fingers on a napkin. Looked toward the high

windows to assess the quality of light outside. Perhaps half an hour had passed since he'd first sat down. There were a few more hours of daylight in which to work.

"And as for my work, I'd best return to it. Please feel free to stay, come and go as you please." He repeated the invitation though he half wished she'd forget he ever made it, would decide she'd had enough of Auldale. He wanted her, and that desire itself was a reminder of everything he wanted to forget.

CHAPTER FIVE

She came every day that week. By Saturday, he looked forward to that moment when the sun was high above, when she'd appear around the curve of the village path bearing nuncheon and her sketchbook.

He met her halfway across the clearing and reached for the heavy basket and then kept pace with her as they walked back toward the castle.

"I told you, you don't need to bribe me with food."

"That's what you say," she said with a laugh. "But I prefer not taking the chance."

Admittedly, he enjoyed the food. While he'd grown used to his simple fare, he was not immune to the charms of a well-cooked meal.

"I wonder what the innkeeper prepares for Sunday dinner. Do you work on Sundays?" she asked.

"No. Actually, I go to church and then join my mother for dinner at the manor."

"John, you shock me!"

He stopped in his tracks, just outside the door of the

castle. He felt the warm brush of Jasper's body against his leg as the dog passed him.

"That I don't work on the Sabbath?" There was merriment in her eyes and he struggled to find the joke.

"That you are positively sociable on Sundays." *Sociable*. The word stayed with him even as she continued talking. "Here I thought you were a misanthropic hermit, and all along, you're simply an eccentric."

His shoulders tensed with irritation. "Perhaps I'm both." He crossed through the threshold, stalked toward the area of the hall that had become their makeshift dining table, and deposited the basket there. He knew more by scent than by sound that she'd caught up to him.

Yes. He knew her scent. He'd likely know it for years, be able to pick her out in the middle of a crowd, even blindfolded.

"I suppose that today being Saturday, sociable isn't in the cards. Shall we settle for roast duck?"

He laughed at that, despite himself. Helped her spread the thick blanket over the cool, time-worn stones.

"Actually, I had thought to invite you to join me tomorrow."

"Had you?" She was smiling at him. As always, that first brilliant flash of teeth, of sparkling eyes, stunned him. "And have you stopped thinking?"

He reached for the loaf of bread. She was in one of her teasing moods. She'd continue this way for a while, he'd learned. Twisting whatever he'd said until she was bored or satisfied.

"Will you?" he pressed. "I can promise you a meal at an actual table. With chairs, tablecloth, and servants."

"Servants, too?" she quipped. "How remarkable."

He sighed. Something had bothered her. He cut a thick slice out of the small truckle of Wensleydale.

"It sounds lovely, John," she said finally, not a tremor of humor in her voice. "But you know I cannot."

He looked up.

"Don't stare at me as if you don't understand," she exclaimed. "You aren't that dense."

She thought him dense? He'd been one of the best at Woolwich. Nonetheless, he did at that moment feel like he was missing something.

"I'm an *actress*. Not a *lady*. I hardly think your mother wishes to break bread with Lord Alverley's former *mistress*."

His cheeks burned hot.

He knew, of course, her history, but it was simply part of who Angelina was. His companion in hiding away from the world. In misanthropy and eccentricity. He laughed.

"It isn't funny."

"I'm sorry," he said quickly. "It's just, I don't think of you that way."

Her face went still, wiped clean, as if she had donned a mask of Angelina and not the expressive woman he'd come to know.

"I know." She made it sound like a failing that he didn't.

He dropped his food down on the napkin. He was losing track of this conversation. She was upset with him now, for more than one reason, it seemed.

"Does anyone else in Auldale know anything about you?" he asked, pushing aside everything else that was unimportant.

She stared and then finally shook her head. No.

"Then come to dinner."

She could imagine that scene. Arriving at the manor and John introducing her to his mother. Mrs. Martin would certainly *not* be pleased. She'd hired a courtesan for her son, not for Sunday dinner.

"But *I* know, John. Your mother will hardly thank you if she ever does discover."

"I find your company pleasant and restful. Why shouldn't she?"

He was just being obstinate now. There was surrender in his voice, acceptance.

She turned to the food. To the slices of roast beef still wrapped in paper.

He'd called her pleasant. Restful. All adjectives that served to make her genderless and asexual. She wasn't a threat to his self-imposed celibacy.

The novelty of it all had its own pleasure. When had she ever spent this many hours with a man with whom she hadn't yet slept? Other actors, she supposed. Or her neighbor in London, Mr. Baswick. He was the fellow who had informed her of the advertisement in the paper. But even that was over the course of months, not days.

At some point, however, this little platonic idyll would end. It had to. She could hardly live forever off the ten pounds Mrs. Martin had advanced her. Really, she should have bargained for expenses paid as well, because the price of the inn and food did add up.

"I didn't mean to offend," he said suddenly, and she realized then how long the silence had dragged on.

She opened her mouth automatically to deny any offense but he continued, not looking at her.

"When you thought me a misanthrope, you were right. I do prefer my own company. Jasper's company."

She had been teasing before. Hadn't meant to hurt him, but he was so serious now, as if her words had had an impact.

"War . . ." He fell off. Took a breath that seemed to physically shake the morose thoughts away. "I enjoy your company too. I appreciate that you make no apologies for your life. Have no shame for your actions. And you have no reason to feel shame."

He stopped but there was so much more in what he didn't say.

"Why do *you* feel shame?" she asked.

He sucked in air sharply. The scar that twisted the left side of his face seemed more pronounced, as if there lay the story, even if he kept playing with the remnants of his food. Even if he never looked at her again. War. He'd started to say it earlier.

The man's realm. She knew nothing of battlefields, other than the fake battles staged with wooden swords on the boards—jealous, spiteful competitors who worked like assassins and puppet masters, doing their damage in shadows.

What had he seen? What had he experienced?

What had he done?

The last thought shocked her.

She'd taken for granted that this man before her was good. His mother's word, his own restraint. The increasing kindness he'd shown her over the week.

But he'd killed men. That was the nature of war. That's how England had vanquished Napoleon.

What else had he done? How had he done it? Why?

He glanced up. Brown eyes dark, pained, even as his lips smirked at her.

She blinked against the stinging, embarrassed by the sudden damp against her eyelashes.

He looked away again, brushed off his pants and stood. Jasper was there instantly in his master's place, scarfing down the remains of lunch as if he thought he only had a moment before Angelina would push him away.

"Running away won't help," she said mildly. She closed the basket and rose to her knees.

"A strategic retreat." His voice was taut, the words an attempt at humor even as he fought against himself. But he wasn't retreating very far. He simply stood there, unmoving, staring at the wall.

She stood as well. Stepped toward him. Touched his arm.

His shirt was made of sturdy cambric, but under her fingers it pressed down and molded to the shape of his muscled arm, which in turn twitched under the press of her hand.

"Tell me," she whispered.

His lifted his right hand, closed it over hers, and looked down at her.

"What did you do?"

"I didn't do anything. That's exactly the problem, Angel." The sweetness of hearing him use the diminutive of her name struck her before she understood the import of his words. And then he continued, "there wasn't anything I could do."

He could see that day as clearly as if it were the present one and he struggled to explain. After the long nights of marking out the ground for the batteries, trudging through rain and mud during the maddening storms, on the night of the attack, he hadn't been in the first assaults on the town. No, it had been other engineers who had led the charge to the breaches by the inky darkness of night. Instead he'd been in the camp, and had seen the blazing lights, heard the distant clamor, the reports that hundreds of British soldiers had fallen.

Thousands, he'd seen later, when, after the city's fall, he'd approached the town.

The trenches were full with those dead and those dying. Death, he was used to, although one never fully became inured to the hell of war, the blood, scent and volume of the violence. And though there had been many sieges, he had not seen devastation such as that at Badajoz.

But it was inside the town that his life changed.

The soldiers had been given leave to pillage, again, a common-enough occurrence in war, but this was different. These were inebriated soldiers fighting each other, murdering civilians, terrorizing and raping the women. After two hours of trying to protect the innocents who were screaming for help, he stood in the middle of the street, feeling as if the houses spun around him. The world spun, and with it the hideous expressions of men he had thought heroes.

Was winning the town worth this?

At least under the French, the townspeople had been spared. Who, then, were the villains?

Sometime during his recitation, they'd moved to the fire, sat down again. Jasper lay by his legs, and he rested his hand on the dog's back.

"These were my friends, men with whom I'd drunk wine and broken bread. Men I had respected and liked."

He glanced at her again, out of the corner of his eye. The horror had faded from her expression. She looked . . . thoughtful.

"You were right. You could have saved one person, perhaps, or two, but not hundreds."

"Thousands," he corrected. But he could see the numbers meant little to her. He saw them in the rows of dead that littered fields or the crushing melee of battle. "And we're the ones who were fighting for what's right. And yet . . ."

"No one protected the innocent."

He nodded.

"That was four years ago, nearly. Why didn't you come home then?"

"Engineers were in demand. I had a duty to England. But when peace came, at last . . . I took my chance." He took a deep breath. "This castle . . . in Spain, on the continent . . . I destroyed things. Here I can build."

"Ohh."

Her eyes were wide, luminous, as if she were looking deep into him. *Understanding.*

A trick of the eye, or more likely, what she wanted him to think. He knew, after these last few days, that only rarely did Angelina reveal any thought or emotion she didn't wish known.

But he *wanted* her to understand. He wanted *someone* to. That, after the last three years, and all these months back home, it would be Angelina, seemed natural. Inevitable.

She reached out, placed her hand over his. Her small, delicate hand. After a moment he turned his own hand and folded his fingers over hers.

CHAPTER SIX

She hadn't intended to go to church. She'd hoped to spend Sunday as she'd spent every other day this week, at the castle. With John.

Who was different from anything she had expected when she'd embarked on this journey. He was a hero. A man who was tall and strong and looked invincible. As if he'd weathered storms. Could make the wind bend to his desire.

But inside, he'd walled himself off as much as he had sequestered himself within the ruins of the old castle fortifications. To protect himself from the ugliness he'd seen at war and the unwelcome knowledge that people were animals and that duty and country and honor could fall away in an instant.

His expression, the language of every curve and line of his body, made the horrors she'd passed over in newspapers into reality.

It wasn't a mistress he needed, but a friend. Someone who would be as solid and true as the rock that surrounded him. As straightforward as Jasper.

Who didn't lie to him. Or intend to seduce him for money.

He'd hate her if he ever knew.

Her chest constricted at the thought.

From a seat in the second to last row of the church, she caught sight of John entering. The ache in her chest grew until she realized she'd been holding her breath, nearly gaping at him.

Half naked, he was a stunning man but this was the first time she'd seen him fully clothed—complete with waistcoat, cravat, coat, and hat.

Devastating. Every man should look like that in his clothes without need of artifice.

His head turned to the left. His gaze caught hers and then he nodded, a slow smile curving the far side of his lips. She wanted those lips. To tease them, run her tongue over them.

She was in a church, for goodness sake!

Oh, Lord. There was his mother standing next to him, watching Angelina leer at her son. Mrs. Martin's eyebrow raised slightly in question but Angelina schooled her features into a neutral expression and looked vacantly through the other woman.

Then John, his mother, and the entire moment moved on. As she had requested, he didn't approach her, nor force an awkward (and unnecessary) introduction.

But seeing him with his mother was enlightening. They shared the same coloring, although Mrs. Martin's dark brown hair was lightened by gray. And as she had the first time they met in London, Angelina itched to suggest coloring it to hide that telltale sign of age. The gray made her nervous.

But where John was tall and broad, with strong, defined features, his mother was petite and wispy, fragile-looking.

Not that Angelina would make the mistake of thinking the woman actually fragile. No woman without iron for her bones would advertise in the paper for her son's mistress. Or perhaps it was foolishness. Yes, if John ever found out, it wouldn't only be Angelina he'd resent. At least the ties of blood might let him forgive his mother.

The church grew crowded. A woman with two children pushed past Angelina into the pew. A farmer's wife, perhaps. The woman gave her a brief, curious look but made no other acknowledgement.

Angelina stifled a sigh and shifted slightly in her seat to catch another glimpse of John where he sat a dozen rows in front of her.

Sunday was always exhausting. John joined his mother in the front right pew. In the front left pew sat Mrs. Ellis and her three young daughters. As usual, John went through the motions, made the necessary comments and noises. But whereas the last two dozen Sundays he'd focused inward, thought of measurements and supplies, today he thought of Angelina. Counted the different shades in her hair, from near white to a sunny gold to a very pale brown. Today, when he'd passed her as he walked down the aisle, that shining mass was pulled up into one of those knots ladies loved. He imagined it down. Wondered how long it was, where the last curl would settle. He looked over his shoulder to catch a glimpse of her. Admired the way she sat, back straight but relaxed, the way her lips moved to shape the words of a hymn or prayer.

A sharp pain pierced his knee and he shifted away from his mother's hand.

"Attend," she hissed.

But the memory of Angelina's pale eyes stayed.

After the service was over, the reverend stopped them, chatted with John's mother. John looked around the emptying church but didn't see Angelina. Disappointment struck him hollowly.

John joined his mother inside the carriage that stood outside, as he did every Sunday, and looked out the window at the familiar landscape passing by as if it were that of Spain or France.

"You are acquainted with that Whitcombe woman who is staying at the inn?" He tensed at the question. Yet, talk about Angelina was inevitable. Gossip traveled quickly in small towns.

"She came to draw the castle," he said, thinking of Angelina sitting on the damp grass, bent industriously over her sketchbook. He still hadn't seen any of her work.

"Ah, just the once?"

"No . . ."

He finally really looked at his mother. There was nothing about her that appeared unusual, but he remembered the earlier sting of her hand against his knee. Her nonchalance was too studied.

"She must be a great artist. You seem to admire her?"

"She's quite lovely," he said carefully.

The gaze that met his was suddenly very sharp and he shifted uncomfortably, as if he were a boy of five and had done something wrong.

"Are you having an affair with her?"

He choked on air.

"Mother—"

"What? How do you think you were born? Your father might be gone these last ten years but I still remember that look. *That* is the look you were giving Miss Whitcombe." She sounded very satisfied. "It is also the look she was giving you."

"Miss Whitcombe is conducting an artistic study of Yorkshire ruins—"

"No." His mother cut him off with a gratingly knowing laugh. "What she is, is an unmarried woman—as I can best tell—who is traveling *scandalously* alone." He wanted to deny it but the words were truth. Of course, what he truly wanted to deny was the tone of his mother's voice, the insinuation that demeaned both him and Angelina. "And while I believe the company in Auldale is all that can be desired, I don't imagine there is much for an *unknown, unmarried woman traveling alone*"—the emphasis his mother placed on those words left no doubt as to what she thought of such a thing—"to find of interest for a week."

I wanted to draw the castle but today . . . today, I just want you. Angelina had said that only five days earlier. It seemed ages ago. But both she and his mother were wrong. What Angelina had wanted, had needed, was a place to retreat, retrench. A place where she didn't have to trade sexual favors.

"We are not . . ." He trailed off under the intensity of his mother's hawk-eyed interest. He wanted to deny everything, because there was no affair. Yet, how did one describe the intimacy that existed between Angelina and him? "This is ridiculous," he finished.

Silence. His mother's expression was unreadable.

"Well, I don't begrudge you it at all," she said at last. "God knows you've risked your life and deserve some pleasure. But I beg of you . . . to not get too attached, or be quite so . . . *admiring* in public. This is Auldale, after all, not London. Scandal does not merely fade away."

He deserved some pleasure? What exactly did that mean? Last week he had taken pleasure in the achievement of his mind and body, the triumph over destruction by man and time. Now pleasure was more complicated. He looked forward to Angelina's visits, to the brief touch of her hand on his, to the look in her eyes when she watched him at work, or when they sat on the floor and shared a meal.

But this other pleasure . . . yes, he wanted it.

The thought, the feeling, had hovered around him this past week, since that first moment he'd seen her kneeling in the great hall, but he'd pushed it away again and again.

Yet there was a pleasure too, in the simple acknowledgement of desire. Even if he never acted upon it.

Yes.

He wanted Angelina.

CHAPTER SEVEN

It was early on Monday when Angelina rounded the curve into the castle's clearing. She was eager to see him but nervous all at once, as if that one day that had passed had frayed the threads between them. She made no pretense at drawing but knocked once on the door for the sake of politeness and then entered, glad that he never thought to lock the doors.

The clattering was in full effect. As quietly as possible, she crossed the hall, placed the basket down and approached the archway to the kitchen. She stood there, leaning against the stone, and watched him. He'd nearly completed the scaffold, would likely have been done if not for her daily distractions. Now he was several feet off the floor, securing a board to the growing frame. He was bare-chested again, only the braces that held up his trousers obscuring the view. She liked watching him at work, seeing those muscles move with each effort. Beautiful. The sort of sight that made her *want* to draw.

Jasper noticed her first, slowly rising from his place in the corner. He came over, panting. Licked at her feet.

Then John stopped hammering and looked down over his shoulder.

She tilted her head to the right and smiled up at him.

His face seemed to brighten.

"You're here early," he called down, making his descent. He leapt to the floor the last couple of feet, startling her.

"Do be careful! I'd hate to think of you being here alone with a broken leg."

He approached. She could see that his hair was damp, as if it hadn't yet dried from the bath. He smelled like lye and exertion. "You'd worry about me?"

"Most definitely," she said immediately. But she knew he was innately competent and self-sufficient.

He leaned his hand against the wall. Desire knotted tightly in her stomach. They were so close, him looming above her, all bare skin and heat. She wanted to press her lips to that skin, to taste that place where neck met shoulder. But she couldn't. Not yet.

"I missed you yesterday."

His eyes were soft, and she melted a bit inside at the gentle tone of his voice. It matched the way she felt inside, the reason she'd forgone her lazing about the inn room and had hurried out to see him. Ridiculous. A silly sentimentality, but there it was.

"Did you have a nice evening with your mother?"

He dropped his hand, ducked his chin.

"I'm almost done with the scaffold," he murmured, as if he were embarrassed. Then slightly louder, "I brought the London papers. By the fire . . ." He gestured with a small wave of his hand.

"Oh!" Excitement overtook every other emotion. She'd purposely tried to avoid thoughts of what was happening in London but she was intensely curious. "Thank you."

He nodded, and turned without saying anything else. She stood there for one brief moment, torn between running to the papers and the idea that perhaps there was more that had to be said. But he was already ascending the scaffold.

She slipped out of the room, settled down by the fire, on the pallet where he had slept just hours before.

As he'd said, there was an assortment of papers, from the *Times* to weekly journals. She skimmed the front pages, down the numerous columns, skipping advertisements and political news. What she wanted was theater gossip, news and reviews.

At the tapping of nails on stone, she turned her head, smiled at Jasper trotting over to investigate what she was doing. He pressed his nose close to her, sniffing, and then turned to the basket of food. He made a little whining sound, and stared at her with pitiful pleading eyes, but she waved him away. He whined insistently a bit more and then finally, tail down, settled down a few feet from the basket.

Back to the paper.

She read a much-delayed review of the Adelphi Theatre's last performance of their season. And then pored over the detailed descriptions of Covent Garden's Shakespeare celebration. The festivities sounded wonderful and everyone had been at the theater that night to see Kemble portray Coriolanus. Kemble could play a witch and people would flock to see him!

A few minutes later Elizabeth Duncan's name was there before her in bold, black ink. Acknowledged by the fiercest critics to be a sensation.

Angelina froze. Heat filled her head. Her skin buzzed. She'd been able to pretend it didn't matter so much, that by the time she'd finished her sojourn in Yorkshire, the episode with Lizzie would have passed and Denham would have moved on to a new lover.

But this—this was different.

She was going to cast up her accounts. She needed air.

"Angelina?" She heard John's questioning voice even as she stumbled from the room, darkness creeping at the edges of her vision.

The cool air was perfect. She stopped where the small rise began its descent, stared southward, toward London.

She breathed deep. It had been foolish of her to pretend that Lizzie Duncan was the only problem. No, Angelina and Denham had parted ways before he'd even noticed the other actress. An amicable split, everyone said, because Angelina had ensured everyone thought so. Because she had gone out of her way to continue flirting with Denham, to point out young women who might appeal to him, so that she didn't look abandoned and desperate.

Which she was.

There was a trick to catching a jaded nobleman's eye and it was to be rare, in demand, unavailable. Three months after Denham handed her her ÿonge, the only man to proposition her had been Fredric Gallant, and he'd done so mockingly. He wasn't even interested in women.

Then the Lizzie situation had arisen, and the flirtatious relationship Angelina maintained with Denham had back-fired.

She felt John's presence at her back although he didn't speak.

John. Who she'd been hired to seduce. Who had turned down her blatant attempts at seduction and resisted her more subtle ones.

She whirled around.

"Why?" She demanded. "You look at me sometimes as if you do desire me, but then nothing. Why won't you touch me?"

Touch me!

He stared at her.

She stepped closer till she was a mere breath away from him. His neck was taut with tension.

"What's wrong with me?" The emotions swirled within her, the anger and despair rising and she wanted to give in, to feel it all in her voice, her body. Let go.

The wind was playing with her hair, whispering against the skin of her neck.

"Nothing's wrong with you."

"Then kiss me."

On the stage, he would have grabbed her. It would have been dramatic and passionate. She would have thrown back her head in mimicry of wild abandon.

Now he stared. And she stared back, daring him.

The touch of his fingers stroking the hair at her temple was warm. Her breath caught in her throat. Then the back of his fingers caressed her cheek.

Kiss me?

She searched his expression, wanting. There were his eyes,

warm, brown, like the earth. Below—the strong lines of his face, the distortion of the scar.

He pressed his palm to her cheek. Her breath rushed out in a sigh, and she let her head rest, lie heavy against his skin.

Closed her eyes. There was that sweet, cool whisper of a spring breeze, the warm strength of his hand, the sounds of his breath. The heat of his—

The first touch of his lips feathered against hers. Gentle, barely more than skin against skin.

She pressed herself against him, reaching up, snaking fingers through the thick strands of his hair as she urged him to deepen the kiss, to give desire a chance.

Desire. The word was like flint, striking flames within her, and suddenly she was aware of the firm muscles of his chest against her breasts, the rough edge of his scar against her lips.

She opened her mouth, sucked him in. His arms encircled her, tightened around her.

Finally.

She slid her hand down, over the bare muscles of his chest. The contact was electric.

She lifted up on her toes.

More.

She was in his arms, her body pressed against him. A wonder. A discovery. She was soft in all the right places. She dragged her teeth over his lower lip, sucked it in to her hot, liquid mouth. His cheek resisted.

Conscious thought catapulted back into his mind. Too aware of his mouth, which no longer stretched with the same mobility as before the wound received at Waterloo, as if after making it through the years of war relatively unscathed, he needed a lasting physical reminder.

He settled his hands on the curve of her hips to push her away but stopped. Pressed his fingers down through layers of fabric. Bare, she would feel lush, silken under his hands.

The way she tasted under his tongue. It was new, strange to kiss, but he had the feel of it now. The feel of her.

Velvet heat. Scrape of teeth, the sharp pleasure of her tongue against his. A surprise. A delight.

He lifted her against him, urged her hips closer to his as he ran his hand down, bunching fabric in his hands, wanting skin, bare, soft skin, wanting the damp heat at the center of her.

"John." Her breath whispered against him and that sensation, too, intoxicated.

He was lost in the folds of her dress, the excess fabric, the barrier of woolen stockings. But he could feel the shape of her legs and they were perfection.

"John." Her voice cut through the haze and he stilled, relaxing his grip, letting her skirts fall back to the ground. He rested his head against the top of hers. Caught his breath.

"I'm sorry," he said finally, reluctantly stepping back. "I was carried away."

She laughed, the sound a breathy, shaky thing. "Oh, I was too. And I don't want to stop . . . but perhaps we could resume inside, by the fire."

He ran his hand through his hair roughly, trying to force clear thought into his head. He wanted to do what she said but something tugged at him. He wanted nothing more than to pick her up, take her inside and lay her down on his bed, strip every single layer of clothing off of her. But with space between them, with the growing clarity of the brisk air, he remembered the way she had looked when she first turned on him. Distraught. This kiss was about more than the passion between them.

She was shivering now, too, without benefit of her coat.

"Let's go in," he agreed.

She smiled and took his hand, leading him back inside. Her hand was light, delicate, and his skin where the pads of her fingers touched him prickled.

She walked slowly, glancing over her shoulder every few feet, shyly and yet seductively. He followed her, questions hesitant on his tongue. He wanted to know what had upset her, but what right did he have to pry?

Yet her distress had made him uncomfortable. Had reminded him that these moments were temporary. Soon she'd leave.

Angelina stopped abruptly before the fire, where the sound of Jasper's snores mixed with the crackling of the burning wood. She turned toward him, running her fingers over his wrist as she did. Then she reached for him with her other hand.

He caught her hand in his, and swallowed hard at her questioning look.

"What happened?" he asked. His stomach was tight with tension.

She pulled his hand toward her, pressed kisses on his fingers, small nips and licks of her tongue that made his body feel alive with sensation. He closed his eyes to savor it. Why was he fighting this?

Still, he pulled his hand away, stepped back.

"What?" she demanded. "Why do you keep stopping? I *know* you want me," she said pointedly. "I *felt* your desire."

A desire still rampant but tempered by this other instinct.

"We need to talk."

He gestured to the floor, to the bed, which was a dangerous place, more so today than it had been during any other of their unconventional discussions. She rolled her eyes but sat. As she lounged there, the hems of her skirts seemed higher, as if she were purposefully taunting him with the curve of her calf.

He sat as well, reaching to the spread-open copy of the *Times* to push it aside.

She laughed, a sound tinged with bitterness, and pressed her hand down flat on the newsprint.

"You wanted to know what upset me," she said.

He looked down at the paper, which her palm obscured, with a sense of dawning understanding. Of course, news of London would not be entirely welcome. He had thought to please her, but the gift had been careless.

She let out an irritated sigh and pushed the paper away. "You have the most overdeveloped sense of responsibility," she complained, as if she had read his thoughts. "It is not *your* fault that I am jealous and petty and cannot bear to hear of that woman triumphing on the stage."

He tried to imagine her as the jealous woman she described, one caught up in a hard-scrabble competition. He knew there had been a desperate sadness to her those first days she had stepped into his life, but she'd relaxed, seemed to take to this strange idyll as much as he had.

"Now," she said, her mood seeming to switch instantaneously from bitterness to seduction. "What did you want to talk about?"

He felt a bit foolish. She had answered his question; what more was there to say?

"Are you intending to reject me again?" she asked softly, incredulously. "Even after that kiss?"

"Angelina."

"Are you saving yourself for marriage? Or is it because I've been with other men?" He listened to her voice ideas that had never once occurred to him. "Or maybe I'm too forward? You prefer to be the one in charge. Is that it, John? You like to be *in charge*?" The way she emphasized those last words hinted at something he could hardly fathom, a world of depravity he'd heard mentioned by drunken soldiers but never explored.

"God, no," he denied quickly. "You are perfect. I . . . I don't want you to feel you *have* to be with me."

She fell silent. Then she laughed, quietly, a sound that ended in a twist of her lips as she studied him again.

"This isn't war," she said slowly. "I'm not a helpless woman caught between armies." The words cut through everything, brought back memories but sliced them through, pushed the fragments to the side. "I know my experience has made me bold and perhaps unusual in my approach, but there is nothing of the usual between us, John."

She closed the space between them, but this time her hand on his skin was simple, a forged bond.

"I am a woman who desires a man, who, I believe, desires her in return."

He swallowed hard. Then nodded once.

"Yes. I do desire you."

The air crackled. His skin burned under her hand. Her own was awake, aware of space and heat. Then space was gone and heat was everything—his mouth pressed to hers, open searching. His arms around her, he engulfed her everywhere.

He was divine. Strong and tall and all hers. She slid her arms up to his shoulders. He swept her up in his embrace. For a moment she was weightless, clinging to him, and then she was lying on the woolen blankets of his bed. The flames in the stone hearth flickered to her left. The scent of fresh straw mixed with wool and the large male who loomed over her, intoxicating her with the touch of his tongue on her neck. After all her attempts to seduce, to take charge, now hardly moving, she reveled in the sensations he wrought from her.

"Angelina," he said, the sound deep, as if he spoke with difficulty. "I want to see your hair down."

She lifted her hand to the messy knot on the top of her head. He rolled to his side, leaned up on his arm, watching her as she pulled out pin after pin. As her hair pillowed unbound beneath her head, he buried his hand in the mass of curls. Even her scalp was sensitive to his touch. She closed her eyes and enjoyed the feeling of his hand playing with her hair. Holding it out to its length and then letting it fall.

"I love your hair. I've wanted to see it down for ages." His voice was deep, thick and she thought he might say more but then his lips were at her temple, soft and warm. A touch that made her want to curl up against him.

"Ages?" she repeated with a laugh. "It does feel as though we've known each other for quite a while, does it not?" Felt as if time had stopped outside this castle, outside of Auldale. As if, at that moment, nothing mattered anywhere else in England. In the world.

Her laughter faded. His eyes were so warm, and she could see the fire reflected in his irises.

"Make love to me," she whispered.

"Hmm." He pulled one of the tendrils of her hair down to her neck. With his finger, traced where it lay on her skin. Then he bent down and she arched her head back as he licked at the spot his finger had been just a moment before. The hum of his voice against her skin was gravelly, low. "I thought that was what I was doing."

CHAPTER EIGHT

The first time Angelina had ever been with a man, she'd been seventeen and relatively ignorant. Oh, she'd understood that men and women were naked together under the blankets, and moved and moaned and made all sorts of jokes to each other that sounded normal but seemed to mean something else that made them laugh riotously. But when she'd lain down with that actor on a pile of hay in a local farmer's barn (how odd, now, to be making love on a pile of hay again), for her part it had been a shy, rough tumble that had left her with a pain between her legs and the idea that suddenly she knew everything.

Of course, she didn't, and when she'd been Alverley's mistress, he'd taught her all manner of sexual relations she'd never dreamed of. It had been laughable what an innocent she still was when she came to his bed.

Here, now, was John Martin, showing her there was still so much to learn.

A man could make love to a woman with the most tender

of touches. Not as a receptacle for his lust, but as another being and body he worshipped with his own.

John's touch was so . . . *reverent.*

"Up with you now," he murmured, his hands on her arms, pulling her to sit. She resisted for one moment, simply to feel completely in his grasp, held up only by him. Then finally, she complied, wondering what would come next.

He shifted, moved behind her. Brushed her hair to the side and pressed his lips—

She gasped at the contact, at the touch of his tongue on the back of her neck. Then she sighed as his hands moved, at the telltale pull of fabric as he undid the laces of her dress. When the neckline gaped he pulled her back against him, his mouth open and hot on her shoulder, his hands delving under the soft muslin, under the stiffer fabric of her stays, the border of her chemise, lifting her breasts to the cool air and his hot hands.

He cupped the flesh, teased her nipples, squeezing them between strong fingers. Sensation ran rivers down her body, pooled at her core, burning, demanding. She twisted in his arms, lifting her mouth to his even as she pushed at his shoulders, wanting him down, beneath her. So that she could taste his skin, straddle him, feel him between her thighs.

She wanted him desperately.

Greedily.

But he was having none of it. Instead he turned her, pressed her down so that he covered her with his body, covered her left nipple with his wet mouth.

The strength of his muscled body against hers thrilled her. He was forceful and demanding, a stark contrast to the tenderness of moments earlier, and she reveled in the change.

She wrapped her legs around him, lifting her hips toward the hard length of his erection.

He growled and she took fierce pleasure in that deep sound. Even more pleasure in his hand running over her stocking-clad thigh. His touch though the woolen fabric made her entire body tingle and then she gasped again, bucking against him, when his fingers passed over the border of her garter to bare skin.

His progress slowed, teasing, and even though his tongue, his lips, laved at her nipples, her focus centered on his fingers' achingly deliberate advance.

Then his fingers were gone, his body gone, and cool air swept in where he had been.

"Your dress," he said, in that low, gravelly voice of desire. She resisted the urge to undress quickly. Instead, she locked her gaze with his and slowly, as slowly as his hand had been on her thigh, peeled off layer after layer, until she knelt before him naked.

He reached for her but she pushed his hand aside.

"Your turn."

He grinned and the flash of his teeth startled her with a glimpse of the boy that coexisted with the man.

He pulled off his boots, and then his stockings and trousers, until he, too, sat naked. If she had ever needed proof of his desire, of his ability to act upon desire, it was there in front of her.

Beautiful.

Their nakedness seemed right in the soaring space of the great hall. Stripped of all its earthly trappings, the luxurious and glittering material goods for which she'd strived the last five years.

She moved into his arms with a sigh, trembling at the feel of skin against skin, at knowing *John* this way.

Reverence.

The word struck her with such power that she clung to him, drew on his heat and strength as she finally understood that look in his eyes. He held her, one hand stroking down her hair, down her back, over and over.

The scent of his skin, his hair, slowly permeated her awareness. His touch sensitized her skin till she was awake everywhere. She pressed her mouth to the curve of his shoulder, tasted him. She was her lips and her tongue, hungry and desirous, needing to know him everywhere, to feel the textures of his body, the hair of his chest, his arms, the hard buds of his nipples, the softer, silkier skin under his arm, at his side, even as her thigh rubbed against the velvet hardness of his arousal.

She moved lower, to the flat plains of his stomach, his hips, where the scent of his desire, his musk, inspired her to descend faster.

His hands on her shoulders were again strong, making her weightless, making the room turn around her until she was on her back, looking up at his face looming over her.

That scarred face, which had been so tight and closed, now open with hunger, with incredible sweetness.

She opened to him, too, her thighs parting to cradle him, her arms outstretched in an embrace.

Then she was open to him in the most primal of ways, his body joining with hers, hard and smooth. She expanded for him everywhere, from the center where their bodies meshed to the tips of her fingers—to her mind, which soared with colors and undulating images, half-grasped words and phrases.

One sentence formed complete—perhaps *he* had seduced *her*—and then she was back to mindlessness, pure sensation, arching to meet his slow thrusts, to pull him deeper.

She wrapped herself around him with a soft cry.

The sound of her pleasure was so sweet and he answered it with his own guttural exhalation. She was wet and burning hot, enveloping him in every possible way. He could stay there forever, deep within her, his face buried in the crook of her neck, breathing in the scent of lilies in her hair. But her hands were exploring his back, his arms, finding places he hadn't known were so sensitive. He lifted himself up, moving again, enjoying the slow build, each retreat and advance. Her neck was arched, chin tilted up, and he drank in the view—the long expanse of her smooth neck, the rise and fall of her breasts as she moved to meet his thrusts, to gain her own pleasure. He wanted to see that pleasure, to see her shudder with it, to feel her squeeze around him as she reached that peak. He shifted his body experimentally and watched the flickers across her face at each small motion.

There. She gasped as he found a new rhythm, his thrusts faster, focused, his hips grinding against hers. She let out little pants, soft explosions of air and her body tensed around him.

"Yes, that," she said. Her hands fluttered against him. "Keep doing that."

He watched the way she fought the sensation at the same

time that she sought it, watched her arch and squirm. She stiffened around him and then her eyes flew open as she softened, her body undulating, pulsing everywhere. He closed his own eyes, holding himself back. *Not yet.* But she felt so damned wonderful.

It had been a long time since he'd last been with a woman, but it would hardly have mattered if he'd had relations even the night before. This was Angelina, beneath him, around him, inside of him as much as he was inside of her. With her body still clutching him tight, trembling, his own trembled.

Then she wrapped her legs around his hips again, and he opened his eyes, saw her lift her arms toward him, watched her perfect lips curve in the most satisfied smile, and he lowered himself to her with a growl. Losing himself until he was just friction and heat and a stunning, shuddering release.

CHAPTER NINE

She lay next to him, naked and languid on the lumpy straw mattress. Her body was beautiful. *Luscious.*

Her eyes were half closed, lips slightly curved. Her chest rose and fell with each even breath—breasts rising and falling—and he enjoyed watching the bluish daylight mix with the reddish flicker of the fire to dance over her skin. His thoughts moved with those patterns of light. Curving, undulating.

He traced his finger around the swell of her breasts, around the nipples. It was still early, just barely after noon. The lumber he'd ordered for the floors and roof would arrive in the morning. Her skin was soft but firm. Along the shadow of her clavicles. Down her chest to the small indentation at her belly. But there was still work he needed to do to prepare.

Her skin was so smooth. He laid his palm flat on the slight downward slope, felt the pulse of her blood flowing mix with the rhythm of his. God, she was beautiful.

His fingers trailed lower, to the damp curls at the apex of her thighs. He glanced back up, found her eyes wide open now, intent. Heat gathered. He felt his body stirring.

But his gaze caught on her leather book in which she had spent hours sketching. He reached for it, untied the knot of the strap. She sat up with a start, grabbing the book away.

"That's mine," she said sharply, all the lovely languor gone.

"Yes, I should have asked," he admitted, settling his hand on her leg instead, stroking the soft skin as if he could coax her back into post-coital gentleness.

She relaxed, set the book aside, and leaned back on her arms. "Keep touching me and I'll forgive you."

He caressed her body slowly, savoring the feel of her firm flesh under his palms. Lowered his mouth to her inner thigh. Listened to her gasp and push at him as if the sensation were too much.

He looked up at her. "I would love to see your drawings. Won't you share them with me?"

She pressed her lips firmly together and looked away. He returned to her thigh, but she was unresponsive now, utterly silent.

"You'll laugh at me," she said finally. "I'm not very good."

He sat up again. "I won't laugh, but I'd like to see Auldale through your eyes."

Her mouth twisted. At last she shrugged and gestured to the book. "If you must."

He hesitated. He'd grown up in a house of women, his mother and sisters, and he knew there were hidden dangers.

"Angelina, if you really prefer I didn't . . ."

She let out a disgruntled sigh, picked up the book and thrust it at him. "You are so bloody noble," she complained. "Just look and see what a fraud I am."

He laughed and opened the book.

And stared. Turned the page, and then turned it again.

She was not being modest. The work was childish at best, the perspective all wrong and lacking knowledge of most basic tenets of art.

"Have you ever studied drawing?" he asked slowly.

"Me? The child of impoverished actors? Hardly." She finished with a laugh.

"Would you like—" He broke off, flipping another page. "I could teach you a bit. Draftsmanship was a requirement at the academy."

She shot him an indecipherable look, although he struggled to understand it. Then she pulled the book away from him again and tossed it to the side.

"I think I might," she agreed, "but for now"—her head tilted flirtatiously—"I'd like to explore a different form of art. Sculpture perhaps." She leaned into him, running her hand down his chest. "You know," she continued, her voice low, "your body is an incredible specimen. So chiseled . . ." She reached lower, and he sucked in his breath at her hand closing around him. "So . . ."

"Yes."

"So yes," she repeated. She was teasing him, he knew. But her fingers were stroking, making it difficult to think of anything but enjoying that touch. In fact, he didn't want to think at all. He watched her hand, pale skin against his, and the sight aroused him even more. Then she ducked her head, and that glorious hair obscured the view but he could *feel* everything. Her lips, by God, her tongue!

He sank back on his elbows, closing his eyes. He was delirious. He'd fallen from the ladder, hit his head and entered some strange, erotic waking dream where everything was right with the world.

And just like that, it wasn't. He smelled smoke and tasted gunpowder. His ears rang, blocking out all other sound. Desperately, he opened his eyes.

Angelina.

She lifted her head, lips curved as if she weren't aware of any change when, of course, it was all terribly obvious. She crawled up to his side, nestled against him, lifted one leg to rest over him.

"I like the way you taste. The way *we* taste."

He twisted to his side, pulled her close, tightly, one hand around her, the other tangling within the masses of her hair.

She was solid and real in his arms.

"Forgive me, I need a moment," he whispered against her hair.

She shifted against him, lifting her head to look at him with those beautiful pale eyes. Unquestioning, soft.

"We have all the time in the world, John," she said. "I'm not going anywhere." She laid her head down against his chest, the softness of her cheek pressed against his heart.

She felt perfect there and for the first time he imagined her staying.

He let out a breath he hadn't known he held.

She listened to the sound of his heart beating fast in his chest. Not all men were ready for a second round of lovemaking shortly after the first. Or maybe there was something else. She didn't know what had happened, but she knew she should say nothing. Let him take the lead.

As her body cooled, her own pulse slowed, the castle took over her thoughts. The castle and the dales outside, the village down the path, the manor a mile away.

In the last hours she'd forgotten why she was there, been consumed with John, with this other world they had created. Now, she remembered with cold clarity that she was employed to be here, to lie in his arms and seduce him toward some future marriage and progeny.

Not imagine staying there indefinitely, as if all those societal trappings didn't matter. As if they were Adam and Eve.

Which they were not.

This was not the Garden of Eden. It was a broken-down castle housing two broken people. *Two?*

She'd flung herself at him earlier, desperate to feel attractive, worthy. To use intimate relations as sustenance. Trying to heal her own wounds the way John's mother had thought a mistress might heal his.

Angelina rolled away, the heat of his body suddenly too much for her, and laid back, resting her head on one arm. She was pitiful.

John had seen that. Seen straight into the center of her, to what she hadn't even known existed. She wanted to scream, or to curl up and die from the embarrassment. She took a deep breath instead, and then sat, reaching for her chemise with shaking hands.

She pulled the loose muslin shift over her head and then let it fall, pool around her hips.

Jasper barked. She glanced to where he stood. He shook himself and then slowly padded over to the basket of food. She laughed, perhaps a touch too harshly. The distraction was welcome and well-timed. Of course, it was likely noon, and the dog had learned in the last week to expect a midday meal.

She crawled toward the basket but stilled at John's hand on her calf. She took another steadying breath. "I'm starving, aren't you?"

She started again, but he didn't let go. Instead she felt him move behind her, his heat nearing, and then his hands were on her thighs, lifting the fabric to her hips. She didn't pull away. This *was*, after all, what she was here for.

The dog whined, as if he sensed his meal would be delayed, but after a glance at his master, he barked once and then slunk back to the corner.

She laughed breathily.

"He'll have his meal later," John said huskily, pressing himself against her, hard and ready, as if he wanted to prove his virility. Not that she'd had any doubt after their last bout. "But what I am starving for is you."

It was the basest of lines, of flirtation, but desire gathered low in her belly, heavy and slick between her legs. She parted her knees, pressing against him even as she looked back over her shoulder.

The look in his eyes stunned her. Made her forget all of her own concerns. He needed her. No, he needed *her*.

What would have happened if his mother had hired some other woman for this role?

"Angelina," he whispered. "Turn over. I want to see your face."

She turned. Lay down again, embraced him as he covered her. Sighed at the sensation of completion as he entered her, at the feeling that his body belonged joined to hers this way. Her heart ached, wanting more, wanting him to fill her with everything that was him.

She curved her hips up against him, trying to still the insidious thoughts. This insanity was the very reason the act was called lovemaking. It should be called love *faking*.

"Angel." The endearment melted her inside. Men had used it before, thought themselves clever or charming, but as with everything John said, there was a ring of sincerity to his words. She *could* love him so easily. If only there weren't her lies between them. But those thoughts were stupidity.

She clung to him, watched his hips undulate against her even as she felt the thrust of him inside her, again and again.

Until he pushed her down, hands on her shoulders, loomed over her, thighs pressed against her thighs, and locked his gaze with hers. He moved within her so slowly it was torture. Delicious torture. She pushed thought aside, focused instead on rhythm and breath, on the sensation building at the center of her with every movement, rising and then rising more.

He was close too. She could feel him nearing his climax as a sharp pleasure within her.

Soon.

Soon.

Then he arched back, crying out, and his voice freed her. She bucked against him, waves breaking over her, shuddering as he collapsed, his breath short pants by her ear.

She closed her eyes and held him in her arms.

CHAPTER TEN

"Can't I help in some way?"

They sat in indolent nakedness, picking through the well-packed basket of food. Apparently the innkeeper had decided to fill it up with what was left over from Sunday dinner. She was hungry, for John, for food, all her appetites awakened. With that hunger was a new energy, a need to be doing. If that doing wasn't naked and sprawled around John's body, she at least wanted to be near him.

"No, you can't help me."

She looked up, startled. "Why ever not?"

"You cannot climb the scaffolding in that dress. It isn't safe."

"Then I'll borrow some of your clothes." When he stared at her with one mockingly raised eyebrow, which matched the eternally mocking slant of his lips, she added, "I shall cinch them very tightly and roll up the legs."

He laughed. "That would be worth seeing."

"You do have other clothes, don't you?" She went over to

his trunk and laboriously lifted the heavy lid. Was *everything* of his oversized? "Ah, yes you do."

He stopped her before she could rifle through the neatly packed clothing.

"Let me."

"As you wish." She stepped aside and watched him bend over, carefully lift several layers of folded cloth as if looking for something specific. He lived so sparsely. Likely life in the army accustomed one to those sorts of habits but, really! How did one do the most basic of things when water must be brought in from the river nearly a quarter mile away and there were no proper kitchens? No kitchen gardens, no pens for chickens or pigs.

He handed her a pair of cream buckskin breeches, quickly followed by a snowy white shirt that looked freshly laundered and pressed. Interesting.

"Do you wash your own clothing?" she asked abruptly.

He handed her braces and a cravat, the last of which she stared at for a moment before realizing he meant for her to use it to cinch the fabric.

He closed the lid of the trunk, stood up straight. "That should do for now."

She didn't move.

"Really, John. What do you do for dinner and breakfast?"

His eyebrows slanted down as if he were perplexed or irritated. "I take care of myself."

"I'm sure you do," she agreed wryly. "But this isn't a farm, and you are out here all by yourself . . ."

"I don't understand why you think I am a hermit."

She laughed. Was he purposefully being obtuse?

"Maybe because you live alone? In a crumbling castle? And you were not very welcoming to me when I first stumbled upon you." The last words tripped on her tongue. More and more she hated the pretense that she hadn't known who he was, that she hadn't come searching him out. It seemed so unfair to him. Although, the time to have told him was likely *before* sleeping with him. Or perhaps she should have had a conscience from the first and never undertaken such a deception. But she'd been desperate. And heartless.

Not that she'd known that or thought about it. That was simply the way things were. One couldn't stop to worry about other people's *feelings* when one needed to compete, to advance, to stay desirable and employed.

What was so different now? Why this delayed sense of right and wrong?

Was it because she'd sunk so low? Her reputation in London ruined?

Or because she cared?

Cared about John.

Of course, she cared about him. Who wouldn't?

"Angelina?"

She blinked. He was staring at her and she'd been lost in thought. Not conscious of what expressions crossed her face. She was losing all sense of herself here in this ridiculous place.

Losing her sanity.

"Well?" she pressed, as if she hadn't wandered off into thoughts better left unexplored.

He laughed, took the pile of clothes from her, and laid it on the chair. Then he pulled her into his arms. Still naked.

"If you were here with me every day, I don't think I'd have any need for laundering at all."

So his thoughts were in the same place. Perfect. Exactly where they should be.

"But when you do have a need?" She pressed closer against him, thigh between his, against the hardening length of him. Had he answered her before when she'd been off in reverie?

"I take them back to the manor. And I bring food from the manor back here. It keeps well enough each week in the storage room, especially with this winter we've had. Sometimes I even visit the manor on a day that is *not* Sunday."

She liked the teasing tone in his voice. It made her want to kiss him. Somewhere. Perhaps right there on his chest, that hollow where the muscle curved.

"If I were a hermit, would you be here with me now?" he continued. She sighed, rested her cheek against his skin. There was the rub, of course. The only reason she was here was because his mother considered him one.

Yes, he was wounded. But Angelina's first assessment had been incorrect. There was nothing wrong with Captain John Martin that time and this castle wouldn't heal.

"You're still upset about the theater," he said softly.

"No, no," she quickly denied, because, while likely she would be when she thought about it later, right then it was the farthest thing from her mind. She stepped away from him, smiled coquettishly, falsely, hiding the truth as she knew well how to do. "I'm simply thinking that I'd better get dressed or I'll never learn how to build a castle."

He laughed, accepting that excuse.

But as she dressed, slipping his voluminous shirt over

her head, the deception lay heavy on her chest. Except for the first lie about why she was here, everything else had been the truth. She rolled her stockings back on. Then stepped into the breeches, which were too long and roomy in certain places, but nearly snug in the hip.

A long, low whistle sounded, and she looked up to find John watching her appreciatively.

She rolled her eyes. She'd dressed in male clothes before, on the stage as Viola in *Twelfth Night*. Still, she liked that look in his eyes.

The one that made him step toward her, grab her close to him, lower his head, his lips to hers. His hands on her backside.

She sighed against him, giving in to the sensation, pushing away the useless guilt. He was enjoying this too. Who cared about the whys?

"I think I should keep you here," he murmured against her lips. "I could use a good laborer."

"Hah!" She pulled lightly on his lower lip with her teeth. "Is that what they call mistresses these days? How very unromantic." She tried to keep kissing him playfully, even as she froze inside at her words, shocked at her lack of thought.

No. Not shocked.

Desperate to tell the truth.

He peeled her away from him. Despite the perpetual smirk, he looked upset.

"You aren't my mistress."

She forced herself to laugh. "No, I'm not, and if you weren't so concerned that I am sleeping with you for all the right reasons, you would have laughed with me."

He still looked terrified.

Nothing that time wouldn't heal.

Her smile faded.

"I lied to you earlier," she said slowly, feeling the air still around them, her words weighted with everything else she could not say. He was truly worried now and she wondered what he feared she would say. "I was neither upset about the castle earlier nor upset about that mess I left in London. I was thinking about you.

"About your wounds."

His wounds. He touched the scar at his cheek reflexively.

"Not that one," she said, the words piercing through him. The back of his neck went hot.

"You are referring to earlier," he said with difficulty. Took a deep breath. He'd never imagined having that problem. But then, in the last few years, lust, desire, sexual relations, had all been rather unimportant to him. "My thoughts wandered." *To how perfect everything was with her.* "To how terrible the world can be. To Badajoz." The one word said it all.

She seemed to be deciding what to say.

"Thank you for telling me," she said at last. "I admit, I did wonder, but I understand. I can't imagine . . . anyone staying . . . aroused . . . amidst such a memory. You must think of it often."

"No." He shook his head emphatically. "I do not. When I work, when I plan, it's far from my thoughts."

"Good." She smiled—tentatively, he thought. "But I wasn't asking about that. I just . . . I didn't want to have lied to you."

He nodded. Caught between the sweetness of her intention and the embarrassment of having misunderstood, having shared more than she had wanted.

"Shall we get to work, then?" he asked tightly, guiding her toward the tower with one hand on her back, toward something that he understood. "We've a castle to rebuild."

Chapter Eleven

She was distracting. From the touch of her fingers as he showed her how to properly hold the nail, to the sight of her moving around in his breeches that molded to her body in a way he'd never imagined breeches would, her presence made his usual focus difficult. Her hips, the curve of her buttocks, her thighs . . . it was ridiculously arousing that she was wearing his clothes.

But aside from the occasional heated glance she sent his way, she did exactly as he said. Eventually they found a rhythm, finishing the scaffolding and starting to lay the wide planks that would form the first floor across the stone vaulting.

"What will you do after you finish the castle?"

Her question cut through the companionable silence and she caught his gaze over the smooth oak plank they carried. Her forehead was damp, with tendrils of hair matted against her skin. This wasn't fit work for her and yet she looked rosy cheeked and alive.

"Hire myself out to other owners of ruined castles. England is cluttered with them."

She laughed. "I believe they call those follies, and they are artfully placed." He laughed too, imagining the shock of a gentleman who discovered his carefully planned picturesque ruin had been "un-ruined."

They set the plank down carefully. When she had stepped back, he adjusted its position to his satisfaction.

"But in all seriousness, John," she prodded.

In all seriousness. He squinted at the encroaching shadows that clung to the walls of the keep.

"I expect it will be many months before I must contemplate such a fate," he said as he stepped back over the plank to where she stood on the scaffolding. "In any event, we have a more pressing issue at hand. It will be dark soon," he noted. "Either you head back now or you stay here tonight."

"How scandalous," she teased. "*My* reputation is not a concern, but I do like a real bed. Perhaps you should walk me back to the inn and stay the night with me there."

"*That* would shock the village." He crouched down by the edge of the wooden platform where the ladder rested. Began the descent.

"Would it?" she called down after him. "What, do they think you a monk?"

"I would hope they don't think of me at all."

He stepped down onto the stone. "Are you coming?"

He held the ladder steady while she descended, enjoying the view of her breeches-clad bottom as she moved carefully down, one rung at a time. If she decided to stay the night, he'd show her again how decidedly un-monklike he was.

"Everyone knows . . . you live out here . . . all by yourself," she said, the words punctuated by short pauses with each movement of her body. "I assure you . . . they are talking. The word is . . . that you are an eccentric."

Chattering fools. So what if they thought him odd? The better that they left him alone.

When she was only a foot off the ground, he reached for her, lifted her into his arms. She fit perfectly there. He rather liked her in his clothes, with none of the concealing fabric of female dress.

She sighed, molding to him. "Not the Golden Lion, then. If I'd known you cared so much for society's approbation, I would never have compromised you."

He pressed his lips to the place where her neck met her shoulder. Tasted the smooth skin. He liked that he could touch her, that he could elicit that small moan of pleasure from her.

"Or perhaps, I would have anyway," she continued. He licked a trail up the side of her neck, wanting to hear her break, to stop talking and moan again. "You know I was determined to have you."

He laughed. She had rather seduced him. Campaigned her way into his bed—the straw pallet she decried as uncomfortable—with stalwart determination. A bit backward, considering that it was the male who was supposed to pursue the female.

As if she'd read his thoughts, she turned in his arms and continued, "I wonder if we'd met in London, amidst the fashionable crowds, if we would ever have started an affair."

He looked down at her face, at the pale eyes that he'd

come to know over the past week, at the strong features of her face, the decisive nose and wide mouth tempered by high cheekbones and a gently rounded chin. She was equally strong, a woman who worked, provided for herself. There was an intensity to her that would be magnetic on the stage. As intensely compelling as he found her here, in the middle of Yorkshire, far away from the sophisticated revelry of London.

In London she'd been part of a society with which he'd never associated, not even as a cadet, spending his breaks at a friend's home in Mayfair.

Perhaps he would have seen her in some play, but he would never have lined up by the stage door, hoping to trade flowers for a smile.

"I think not," he said finally, even though none of it mattered, because that alternate world did not exist. Events had shaped him, had shaped her, and here they were now. Lovers. Something wonderfully bright arisen out of the darkness.

Even though the light outside was fading, he found himself expanding as if it were morning, the first rays of sun urging his eyes open.

"I suppose you wouldn't have deigned to look at an actress?" There was a tone in her voice that made him wary and she stepped back out of his embrace. "Or perhaps it is your antipathy to have a mistress? Why is that, John? Why can I not be your mistress?"

The word itself bothered him. But she was upset and he struggled to understand why. Not that he wanted to discuss it at all. He wanted to kiss her, to hold her again, to breathe in her scent.

"You said quite clearly" ––he remembered her mocking

expression— "that you were completely uninterested in being *kept* by me."

"And then you tried to convince me of how wealthy and consequential you are."

He let out a small embarrassed laugh.

"Does it disgust you?" she pressed, shocking him with the very idea. "That I've been with other men. That they've *paid* me?"

Her expression hardened as she challenged him, and for the first time he wondered what *she* thought of her past. He'd thought her proud of it, matter-of-fact. He'd accepted it as part of her, as much as everything that he had done was part of him.

He struggled to put into words that which he knew instinctively.

"Angelina, we came to each other as equals. You owe me nothing." She seemed to soften a bit, as if curious. "Our relationship is pure."

"Such a romantic!" The words were mocking but she swayed toward him, shaking her head. "What am I to do with you?"

Finally, a question for which he had an answer.

"Stay the night."

Chapter Twelve

She snuggled under the woolen blanket, curved against John's body. His chest rose and fell rhythmically, and she'd matched her own breath to his. It was early yet, the sky still dark and the fire now merely glowing red embers in the hearth. She could just make out Jasper's outline at the foot of the mattress.

In that dim light, John's body, too, was a dark shadow. A bold shadow in the foreground, if she were to draw this scene. And then, if there were a bit more light, she would be able to see the table in the middle of the room, which would form the middle ground—the *spirited*, John had said. Last, at the far end of the great hall, was the stone wall, which so begged to be covered by some medieval tapestry. The wall would be fainter, *delicate*, to establish its distance.

She rather liked the bold part the best. Especially as that large recumbent form was so enticing to her lips.

How quickly she'd grown used to this—to the touch of his skin, to his scent and that of sleeping by the hearth. To the feel of the straw mattress lain over stones.

Three nights. Three beautiful days and nights in which she'd spent nearly every waking moment with him. Except for the brief mid-morning hour that she'd returned to the inn, walking past the innkeeper's wide-eyed stare at her bald return after an absent night, to gather some clothes and toiletries. If the village hadn't been gossiping already, she'd just given them cause. An unfortunate unintended consequence of Mrs. Martin's plan, for what respectable local woman would hear these rumors and not misconstrue John's character?

He'd be branded a *rogue*.

She smiled against his shoulder. As a lover, perhaps, he *was* shameless, and surprisingly excellent. In everything else, she'd never known a *less* roguish man.

In fact, he was everything honorable and good. The proverbial knight in shining armor, willing to slay dragons for a damsel in distress.

Even if she wasn't quite in distress.

In some other play, she'd stay here in his castle, be beloved by him. *Love* him. Even the word itself made her chest tighten. Plays of love, where all ended well, were not particularly fashionable at the moment. Skewering wit and social commentary, or at least a good tragedy, were far more favored among the populace. Accordingly, her life was more of a Sheridan play.

She slid away from him, stretched out, and stared up at the royal blue light of a night about to break into day.

So she loved him. What did she know of love? This was nothing like that first desperate infatuation of her youth, when all she cared about were *feelings* and dramatic gestures.

It was nothing like the sophisticated flirtations and meaningless companionship of her time with either Alverley or Lord Peter.

With John, she'd stripped naked, beyond her literal skin, down to the parts of her she rarely, if ever, acknowledged to herself. Terrifying.

Thrilling.

There was more to each touch, to each kiss, to the feel of him entering her, holding her tight in his arms. There was passion but it had depths she'd never known before. That she'd never imagined existed.

She cared for John, but not only as her lover or her keeper. In fact, he'd hate that she ever thought of him that last way at all.

Oddly, he was her friend.

The sound of a rooster cut through the morning air and the thick stone walls as the first light shimmered silver into the room.

John stirred next to her, reached for her with his eyes half open.

"Morning already?"

She rolled into his embrace. Slid her body against his, over him, one thigh slung across his legs, against the hardened length of him.

"No, still night," she whispered. "Until I wake you up properly."

She straddled him, forgoing foreplay, forgoing anything but the satisfying slide of his body into hers.

"You spoil me." His face was still soft from sleep and the

distortion of the scar less pronounced. He looked relaxed. Happy.

"You deserve to be spoiled." She moved over him slowly, bending down to lick the hot skin of his neck, to feel her sensitive breasts graze against the wiry hair of his chest. Pleasure unfurled within her and she watched that sensation matched in his expression. "You are such a beautiful man."

"Men aren't beautiful," he said gruffly, resting his hands on her hips, taking control.

She laughed. "Said by a man, of course. If you could see yourself through my eyes . . ."

"Through my eyes, all I see is you." She let out a small sound of surprise as he lifted her and flipped her onto her back. But he was over her, thrusting in again, deep, before she had recovered her breath. Then his mouth covered hers and she didn't care about anything but the sharp feel of his tongue against hers, the way he electrified her body. "Stay."

Had he spoken or was it simply her own thoughts echoing in her head?

"Angel, stay here with me."

She lifted her hips, urged him on toward his completion, her thoughts galloping wildly away from her own.

She stroked his skin, lifted her hips up to meet his, squeezing her thighs around him, around this male body that mingled with hers.

What did he mean? Stay the morning? The night? A month? Stay forever?

He stilled over her and then his hips rocked again and again as his body shuddered. She held him close, tight.

No, of course not forever. She could just imagine his mother's delight to find the woman she'd hired had settled in, had destroyed any hopes of a respectable marriage for her son, of grandchildren.

God, his mother!

Angelina cringed inside. Here she was imagining some lovely eternal idyll by his side, when all of this was built on a lie.

A lie constructed in order to do a job.

Which she'd done.

A cold awareness spread through her. If she did stay, whether for hours more or a day, this attachment they felt toward each other would only grow. She'd been hired to *heal* John, not to hurt him.

Not to hurt herself.

She had to go.

Now. This morning. As soon as she could gather her belongings and find transportation away from here. Back to the London Road. Back to London.

Yes. London.

Forget York or Bath or any other place. She'd face down the shame, grovel at Lizzie's feet. The wench would like that.

John's body was heavy over hers but she savored the feeling of him there, wishing she'd known only minutes before that this would be the last time.

Not that it really mattered. When she was away, in London, this lunacy would pass. She'd forget the last eleven days as easily as she'd forgotten Alverley.

Jasper stood, shaking himself. She smiled at the sight of the dog padding down the hall to go outside.

"It's morning now, darling," she said lightly.

John laughed, but rolled off of her, cool air rushing in where the heat of his skin had been.

"That eager to finish the first floor?"

"Actually, I need to go to the Golden Lion. I believe Mr. Garrett will think I've absconded and sell off my belongings."

"I'll go with you." Of course, this day, after all the other days when she would have been glad for company on the walk to and from the village, he would decide to break his isolation.

"As much as I'd love your company," she said quickly, forcing herself to meet his gaze with a teasing glance, "there are some things a woman must do for herself." There, that was suggestive enough that he should assume some mysterious female business where men were decidedly unwelcome. But it was not a lie. *Not* a lie.

"Perhaps there is something I can do for you before you go," he said, reaching for her again. She melted into his embrace.

Once more, then. For remembrance.

She'd sent a note, as discreetly as possible, to the manor house, hoping that news of this meeting would never reach John's ears. It had been one thing to meet with Mrs. Martin at a hotel in London, where no one knew either of them. It was entirely more difficult to arrange such anonymity here in Auldale. Thus, she was waiting in the woods, not far from the manor, and hoping this interview would be short.

The weekly market would be over soon and as kind as Mr. Brown and his wife were for agreeing to take her as far as the

London Road, she could not be certain that they would wait for her if she were to be late.

It was strange to stand barely half a mile from where John, unaware that she wasn't coming back, continued to work. What would he think when he realized? Maybe it was cruel to leave without a word. Perhaps she should have come up with some excuse, but she couldn't bear to lie. And she couldn't tell him the truth.

"Miss Whitcombe." There was Mrs. Martin. Angelina took a deep breath and met John's mother halfway. This was a meeting very different from that one three weeks earlier. Three weeks! It felt like years, like some strange suspension of time. "I admit, I'm surprised to hear from you this soon."

She forced herself to smile, to act as if this situation were commonplace. As if this were not the mother of the man she—

"I can assure you that your son is competent as far as women are concerned."

Mrs. Martin had the grace to look embarrassed. Where had her finer feelings been when she'd decided to meddle in her son's life?

"Excellent." Yes, most excellent. Wonderful, in fact. Everyone should celebrate because Angelina had managed to seduce a man. She needed to leave and she wanted her payment. To put all of this behind her as soon as possible. But Mary Martin stood there, hands clasped in front of her as if there were more she wished to say.

"Yes?"

"In your . . . professional opinion, Miss Whitcombe, do you believe my son is ready to pursue a wife?"

The other part of Angelina's task. But how could she ever promise such a thing? She pulled her coat close around her, stalling her response. If her financial situation weren't quite so dire, she'd act on her conscience, refuse the balance of the payment. But she didn't have the luxury to make such a choice. And yet . . . *John.* His name was a sigh in her heart, a sadness for something she couldn't possibly have.

"My profession has nothing to do with it," she answered finally. "There's nothing at all the matter with your son. I presume when he is ready to marry, he'll undertake such an endeavor."

"But he was wounded!" Mrs. Martin insisted, "I explained to you—"

"And he's still wounded, ma'am. No amount of sexual relations or female influence will change that." At the alarmed look in John's mother's eye, Angelina let out a harsh, frustrated breath. "I do believe I brought him some comfort."

"You think I'm a foolish woman, aging and losing my senses."

"It isn't my place—"

"No." Mrs. Martin drew herself up. She looked peevish and irreversibly proper, although her meddling actions were hardly the sort of behavior of any respectable lady. "It *isn't* your place. And I cannot say I'm happy with your report."

A frisson of alarm crept down Angelina's back.

"You don't intend to pay?"

Mrs. Martin pressed her lips tightly together.

"I shouldn't. Certainly not one hundred pounds . . . but I am a woman of my word and I hope that I shall find you have been as well." She took her purse from her dress, withdrew a folded banknote, which she held out gingerly.

Mrs. Martin found this whole business distasteful. How amusing.

"I wish him all the best," Angelina said, accepting the money with a tight smile. She turned to leave and then stopped, unsettled. She had to say something. She looked back over her shoulder to find Mrs. Martin hadn't moved, was staring after her with a thoughtful expression on her face.

"Mrs. Martin?" The other woman raised one questioning eyebrow that reminded Angelina of John. She swallowed hard. "Please, no more schemes. Give him the space he needs."

CHAPTER THIRTEEN

At noon, John climbed down the scaffold and walked back into the great hall. Empty still. Of course, she'd only left two hours earlier. Perhaps she'd wanted a proper bath, or had letters to write, or some other business to attend to. It was market day as well. She hadn't actually said she'd be back in time for the midday meal to which he'd so recently grown accustomed.

It was nearly three when he dressed properly and then started down the path himself. The market would be over by now, but he needed more nails. Or he would eventually need more nails, and it was just as well to be prepared ahead of time.

Or maybe . . . maybe he wanted to make certain nothing had happened to Angelina. As safe as Auldale usually was, it *was* market day. Or perhaps she'd tripped on a downed tree. He should have cleared this path days ago, or accompanied her every time she went back to the village.

A bit late for the concern.

Not that anything *had* happened to her. This was Auldale. Peaceful, dull corner of Yorkshire. In fact, Angelina was the only stranger. Not that she was a stranger to him anymore. How could she be when he knew what made her laugh and what made her smirk? When he knew intimately every inch of her body? Knew about her childhood, her past lovers, and her dreams for her future?

Her future. That was why he was uneasy, swallowing up the countryside with vigorous strides.

She'd said nothing that morning. No acknowledgement that he'd said anything at all.

She eventually wanted to go back to London and the noisy, exciting life she'd described, back to the stage.

He wanted her to stay. Stay indefinitely. Move all her belongings to the castle and give up that room at the inn. Make *eventually* some very distant time.

Foolishness. He'd known her for all of two weeks. Not even that.

Yet, he did know her. Better than he'd ever known anyone else.

And he was damned sure that she cared for him too. Only, she'd hidden everything underneath that flirtatious smile, and he'd let her.

The inn was busy for Auldale, filled with a half dozen tradesmen and locals sharing drinks after the morning's work. Mr. Garrett, the innkeeper, spied John and ambled over.

"Afternoon, Captain." John winced at the honorific. But it was a measure of the villagers' respect that they didn't return to the simpler Mr. Martin. "It's always a pleasure to see you, but if you're looking for the miss, she left a few hours ago."

"Miss Whitcombe?"

Garrett nodded, looking a bit uncomfortable.

"Said she wanted to catch the coach on the London Road. Brown and his wife took her up in their wagon."

"Miss Whitcombe left?"

"Yes, Captain," Garrett said slowly, as if he needed to enunciate each syllable to make certain John understood. But enunciation wouldn't make him understand. The meaning of the words was incomprehensible. Inconceivable.

Why?

And so abruptly, without a word?

"Thank you, Mr. Garrett," he said perfunctorily before leaving. Before making the other mile-long walk that was 45 degrees radially from the path to the castle. The walk to the manor and to the stables.

He could catch up to a farmer's cart easily.

As he crossed the curved cobblestone drive of the manor house, the front door opened and his mother stepped out, waving to him. As if she'd expected him, had been waiting by the windows for him to show up.

"Georgie! What a delightful surprise!"

"John, mother. Please," he said reflexively, even as he passed her. He could hear her scurrying to catch up with him. Frustrated, he slowed his pace.

"You were named George for a reason, dear, like your father."

"Actually, you named me Hubert, but neither of us prefers that moniker."

"Well, that was simply to appease your grandfather. What a wretched man. He always refused to be happy for your father and me. In any event, I am so happy you are here and I don't have to hunt you down at that dreary pile of stones. I am having a dinner tomorrow night and I would like you to attend."

"No."

"Georgie!" He could hear that tone in her voice. The one that signaled impending tears. His younger sisters had always been able to ignore it, but he never could. "I rarely ask anything of you!"

He threw open the door to the stables, into the scent of animal and fresh hay. The stable boy jumped out from the stall he'd been mucking. The groom, Charlie, was nowhere in sight.

"Saddle Hal." The bay was the fastest in the stable. And at the moment, he valued speed over stamina.

"Where are you going?"

Finally he turned to his mother. She looked the same as she always did, a pale patterned cap over her curls, a style she had worn for the last decade.

"For a ride." To stop the desperation that had circled around him ever since Garrett had said Angelina was gone.

"Forgive me, *John*," his mother said with an arch edge that startled him, "but you haven't been on that horse in three months. Today, that woman leaves Auldale and you suddenly want to take a ride . . ."

"Does everyone know?"

She laughed. Then cut the sound short.

"You didn't know she was leaving?"

He was not having this discussion with his mother. He glanced to the stable boy, who was taking an excruciatingly long time to do a simple task. One that John should have done for himself. He pivoted on his heel, strode toward Hal, who was standing patiently as the boy took his own sweet time about saddling the horse.

"If she didn't tell you she was leaving, don't you think she had her reasons?"

Yes, he damn well hoped Angelina had excellent reasons. He wanted to know them. Needed to.

Stroking the horse's head, he gestured to the boy to step aside.

"John!"

The bay lifted its head toward the noise. John moved to the stirrups and adjusted their length. Why wouldn't his mother go away?

"You cannot go after her."

"I can."

"And do what? Bring her back to stay? Forever?" He rubbed his thumb down the raw edge of the leather straps. "It's one thing to have an affair, dear, but to flaunt it in front of everyone in Auldale?"

Stay. That morning, forgetting all the restrictions of society, he had asked Angelina to stay.

He dropped his hand to his side. There was no point in his going anywhere.

This was her answer.

CHAPTER FOURTEEN

London had changed. Somehow in the handful of weeks that she had been away, the city had shrunk, become more crowded, more stifling.

As if there were no place for her any longer.

Not at the theater, where she had borne Lizzie Duncan's caustic wrath with a great show of humility. Even groveling could not add more dates to the theater's season or inspire the manager to replace anyone. He had, however, offered her a small part in a melodrama at a minor theater in which he had an interest. The sort of role she had not taken even in her first days in London five years earlier.

While she'd accepted the employment with gratitude, it was much more difficult to accept the small attic chamber Mr. Baswick was now showing to her.

Her old landlord looked entirely unchanged—same paunch at his waist, sagging jowls, thinning gray hair, same garrulousness and eagerness to gossip—and yet, like London, he seemed different.

"What, did you expect me to leave your previous rooms

empty indefinitely? You know that Maggie Shelton has been wanting a space in the house for years. Maggie's expecting again." He added the last in a twinkling-eyed hush.

"I suppose I hadn't thought I'd be here again," she admitted.

"But you'll take it."

She smiled at him wryly. "Yes, Bas, of course I'll take it. You're my one friend in London."

"That's a shame," he said. "A pretty girl like you. But come on then, as friends let's have a cup of tea and you can tell me about your sojourn in the wilds of the countryside."

She followed him down to his own apartment, where she'd spent the occasional afternoon playing a game of piquet over sherry-spiked tea. At least the many flights of stairs no longer winded her quite as much as they would have before Yorkshire. Many more of those daily walks and she would have been as hardy as a country girl. As she'd once been in her youth.

"I spend my days posting advertisements and fielding letters for advertisers," he continued, huffing as they descended the three flights. "But never do I get to hear the stories that happen after a match is made, if a match is made. So tell me, what was the problem with the young man that he needed his mother to hire his mistress?"

She laughed. Bas might have been the one to tell her of the advertisement and she was grateful to him for his help, but there was very little of the story she was willing to share.

"He didn't know," she said, settling once again on part of the truth. He whistled through his teeth. "And, as of the moment, he still doesn't know. For his mother's sake and his,

I hope it stays that way." For her own sake too. Better to be remembered at least somewhat fondly, even if he would resent her for her abrupt departure. "But enough of *Yorkshire*. What we really should talk about is all the gossip I've missed while away."

When she was alone in her room, her sole trunk placed at the foot of the narrow bed, she took a deep, steadying breath. The room was small even by London standards, but at least it was inexpensive. She'd learned her lesson about frivolous spending and debt.

There was a small window, which overlooked the bustling street. She had always thought that activity exciting and vibrant. But through that opening, the stale air of the city wafted in.

She missed fresh air and freeing space. She missed all the colors of the countryside. She missed that collie sticking his wet nose in her face.

She missed John.

The house was stifling, the company insipid. The dinner party at the manor house was proving to be even more unbearable than he'd imagined it would be, as his mother apparently intended to play matchmaker. Whether it was sandwiching him between the two young Treythorn sisters, who had both been children the last time he'd seen them, or forcing him into a conversation with their cousin Miss Cooke, his mother made little attempt to hide her goals.

He shouldn't have come, but nights at the castle had

grown increasingly unbearable. Everything reminded him of Angelina. He had known her for less than a fortnight and yet she'd changed everything, unsettled the tenuous peace he'd found.

He should never have let her into his life.

Not that he had. She'd sat outside his home as tenaciously as an army at siege. Out of boredom, he assumed. An ennui that had changed to something more.

Working on the castle, he'd done well not thinking about war, about people, about his antipathy for the destructive force of human nature. But he could not stop thinking about Angelina. Tortuous thoughts snaked through his mind as he struggled to answer the burning question, "Why?" But always he circled back to the truth that he would never know the answer, and that neither the question nor the answer mattered.

John weathered the evening, parrying the lightly barbed inquiries into his activities with as much humor and goodwill as he could muster. After all, Angelina had been somewhat right about his isolation, at least in regard to the local society. He hadn't suffered one of these engagements since the second month he'd been home, when his mother had insisted on feting her returned hero son.

His mother's sidelong gaze bored into him the whole night, as if he were an insect to be studied under a microscope.

How did everyone else go on as if nothing had changed? As if the peace had always been so? As if Angelina had never entered his life and left?

The night continued seemingly interminably until one by one his mother's guests, people he ostensibly knew, stepped out of the house and into their carriages, back to their own homes.

To whatever private lives they had.

"You must make more of an effort, John," his mother said when the last guest had gone.

More of an effort.

"They are my neighbors, not my friends."

"Those neighbors comprise the entirety of eligible young ladies in the area. You are eight and twenty, John. Eight and twenty. It is time to marry."

Angelina. Her image blossomed in his mind. He had thought himself far from matrimony, far from ready to consider sharing his life with another, but she, he could have loved as a wife.

If she hadn't left.

Maybe he should have followed her. It had hurt to be abandoned, to have had her disappear with no word, but she must have had good cause. Perhaps an excellent reason that didn't include *wanting* to leave. An insidious thought.

"What if I married Miss Whitcombe?"

His mother's eyes flew open wide and she looked for a moment like she would choke on air. Not a fortuitous sign.

"The woman with whom you were carrying on an affair?"

The last time she had suggested he and Angelina had been conducting a liaison, he had truthfully denied it. Now he could not. He nodded.

"She's not . . . she's not acceptable, Georgie." He winced at her return to his childhood name, to the tone of tentative condescension in her voice. "Not the sort of woman one marries. In any event, she's gone."

Gone. Yes, he knew that, but some devilish obstinacy made him press.

"I find her infinitely more acceptable than any of the women you paraded before me tonight."

"What, you think your Miss Whitcombe is all that is virtuous?" his mother demanded incredulously. "That somehow she's better than any other woman?"

Better for him. Not that it mattered. God, he missed her. How fast she'd upended his life, made him need more. Need her. Did she even think of him now, wherever she was?

"She's an actress. A *prostitute*." His mother stood there, passing judgment. As if anyone had the right. He knew Angelina and his mother did not.

"Yes. But she's honest."

His mother laughed derisively.

"Honest?" she repeated. "Do you even know why she sought you out? I can see you don't. I hired her. To *be* your mistress. How honest is that?"

Heat turned him to molten stone, fury rising within him.

"You did what?"

His mother lifted her chin, standing her ground.

"I employed Miss Whitcombe."

"To be my mistress?" *His mistress.* Angelina had been his mistress. Been paid to love him. Had—

He reached out blindly for the wall, staggering for its support. Dear God, what was truth and what was a lie?

"*Why can I not be your mistress?*"

"*Are you trying to entice me to seduce you?*"

"I'm not in the market to be your mistress."

She'd been mocking him, laughing at him. Using him. Of course, she had left!

Had she even loved him?

Not that she'd said she had but that last morning, it had felt . . .

He was an idiot.

"I only did it because you can't hide yourself away in that pile of stones for the rest of your life. It isn't normal or healthy." Would his mother not stop talking? Leaning, back against the wall, he stared at her as she spoke. Her lips moving, the words floating over him in a continuous wave. The way air felt after an explosion—hot and fast and so deafening the world was almost devoid of sound. "And do you know what people say? Georgie, it's time to move back home."

"No," he said finally, finding his voice, finding clarity of purpose within the roiling emotions within him. "It's time for me to go to London."

CHAPTER FIFTEEN

It was only when he was ascending the staircase up to the fourth floor of the narrow boarding house that it struck him how remarkably easy it was to find Angelina in London. The largest piece of luck being that she had taken rooms at the same house in which she had resided before her sojourn in Auldale.

As he climbed the last flights, he slowed, his legs leaden, a strange nervousness overtaking him. What was he doing?

He'd let fury—the sense of betrayal and the need for answers—propel him to London. But now, ten steps from seeing her again, none of his excuses made sense.

He stopped abruptly.

Jasper bounded up past him, panting with the effort. He watched his dog scramble up onto the landing and then look back, as if to say, *Well?*

Yes, well.

Why was he here?

Because she'd lied to him. Because he wanted to know

who the real Angelina Whitcombe was. Because she didn't get to make him love her and then walk away without consequences.

Knock on that door, Captain.

He stood taller, finding a strange comfort in the experiences he'd struggled to forget.

As if he were going into battle.

He took the steps two at a time. Swallowed the length of the hallway in half a dozen strides.

Knocked on the door.

The wood felt flimsy beneath his gloved knuckles. One strong rap and he could break it down, tear the inadequate lock from the jamb.

Which meant anyone else could.

The neighborhood was respectable enough, but London was London and she was a woman living alone.

He raised his hand to knock again when he heard the sound of footsteps, muted by the door.

The door opened and there she was. The same and yet different. Harder, smaller. As if London had leached color from her skin, the sunlight from her hair.

But those eyes were the same, and as they widened in incredulous recognition, she seemed illuminated from within. The way she'd appeared—

"What are you doing here?"

Then she looked down, and he looked down, too, at where Jasper was pushing his face up against her dress, trying to climb the fabric up to her face.

"And you too," she said with a breathy laugh, before looking up again. "This . . . is a surprise. Would you . . . like to come in?"

As if Jasper understood the question, he pushed past Angelina into the room beyond.

Still John couldn't find words to answer her. This was not battle. It was surrender.

"Do you love me, Angelina?"

There was no past, no future, nothing but the present. The space between them. The dim light of the hallway. The worn wood of the floor.

Her mouth parted and she lifted one hand to her lips.

"Yes. But—"

"Yes. Stop. That's enough." He closed his eyes, aware dimly that he was nodding, as if repeating that confirmation. "All right." He took a deep breath and opened his eyes. "Then why did you leave?"

Two weeks she'd dreamed of him, seen his face, his naked body, like a vision in the dark of the night. She'd caught his scent at strange moments, stopped still on the streets beset by memories, immobilized by the ache in her chest. Now he was there, standing on her doorstep, wanting answers. She shouldn't have admitted she loved him. That was a mistake. But he'd startled her, caught her off guard. And for heavens' sake, she *did* love him.

But however he had found her, for whatever reason he had come, she still couldn't tell him why she'd left. A partial truth, then. Again.

"I left *because* I fell in love with you. If I'd stayed any longer, leaving would have become even harder."

"Or did you leave because you'd done the job you'd been hired to do?"

"Ah. So you know." She smiled thinly. "And you tracked me down to excoriate me?"

He was silent. Staring at her, his gaze demanding and relentless.

He wanted to know. Fine. No more lies, no more half-truths.

"I left because the job was done and there wasn't any point in staying. I loved you but what was love when based on a lie? It wasn't my place to tell you I'd been hired."

Her breath released in a shudder.

Still he was silent. He'd never been a man of excess words but this was unfair. He had to speak, not just stand there with that false smirk taunting her.

"You have every right to be upset. I seduced you for money. I accepted that money even after I fell in love with you. I lied to you." She put her hands on her hips. "But I only lied to you about why I was there. Everything else . . . everything else was the truth. Not that I wouldn't have lied. If you'd been some other man, I'd likely have felt no compunction then. But everything was different between us. So there is your answer. Satisfied?"

"No, I'm not satisfied," he said finally, the words a low growl.

"What do you want from me, John?"

"I want you to come back with me."

"To Auldale?" She laughed. "Are you finally, at long last, asking me to be your mistress?"

"No, I'm asking you to be my wife."

Oh.

Oh.

She turned around and walked over to the bed, where Jasper had taken up residence as if he lived there. She moved his tail aside and sat down.

John shut the door. She could feel the room getting smaller. This tiny attic apartment with its slanted ceiling was no place for a man of John's height. John. Who had just asked her to *marry* him. The last thing she had ever expected him to say.

She had put away thoughts of marriage when she'd taken up with Alverley. Oh, someday maybe. But only three months ago she'd been in the prime of her career, rising through the ranks. Another year and her name would be as known as Siddons. Well, perhaps not Siddons.

Until everything had unraveled.

Then transformed.

And now—*Marriage?*

And why wasn't he furious, incensed, raging about her heartlessness? She would have, had the tables been turned.

"If I say yes," she said slowly, looking up at him, "I could be wealthy, settled. I'd be your mistress in another way entirely, even if we call it wife. Is that what you want?"

"I want *you.*"

Those words had power, even now when she was confused, upset. He was so very much *him.* This was her stoic lover, away from his castle, away from where he'd shut himself away.

And in this attic room, which was so opposite of everything that had been between them, she wasn't the woman he had called Angel in the middle of the night.

"You are willing to defy society and your principles, compromise your mother's happiness to achieve such a goal? Don't you care at all?" she demanded. "That I've been a mistress. I've loved men for money. That I've been *your* mistress, John?"

He shook his head slowly.

"Why are you saying these things? Tell me no, if that is your answer. Why try to ruin everything that was between us?"

A desperate anger swelled up inside her. She knew he didn't care. He had never cared. She knew as well that many men of property had married actresses, married their mistresses even. But what would their life be like in Yorkshire? It was not London, where, if perhaps not commonplace, such a union was not entirely strange. In the small village of Auldale, would their love be accepted?

She couldn't think clearly. There were too many thoughts, too many reasons why this was wrong.

"Because it's not fair!" She stood up and faced him, her hands fisted, her body trembling.

"It's not fair that I love you?"

"It's not fair that you are decent, and kind, and that I met you the way I met you. And that I have to live with that. If I marry you, I'll have to live with your mother knowing that. The world isn't that idyll we had. It's bigger."

She was angry but hope sprung in him at her words. Everything she said was true. Their past existed. He'd come to

London furious but that emotion had seemed irrelevant the moment he'd seen her again. The moment he'd known he still loved her.

She was standing in front of him, shaking, and he wanted to take her into his arms. Hold her, breathe in her scent and feel the comfort of her body against his. But that wasn't what would convince her to trust him.

"You are right," he agreed. "Life would not be easy." She cocked her head to the side and he noted that her hands had unclenched. He pushed on, finding his way to her. "But it would be an idyll. With you. If you prefer London, then we'll live here. Wherever you want to be."

"London?" She looked incredulous again, but at least here by the light of the window, he could see the pale blue of her eyes. "What about your castle?"

He laughed. "Well, I would hope it does not have to be one or the other."

She laughed as well, *with* him, and the tension inside him lightened.

"No. It doesn't. Although I can't imagine I'll be on the stage anymore."

She had asked once what would have happened if they'd met in London. He would have seen her act then, most likely. Had a chance to see her in her element. He'd been wrong before when he'd said they would never have been lovers. He would have loved her at once.

"Will that upset you?"

She pursed her lips, thinking. "Not really, I suppose. Live in an attic and work at bit parts for years until someone takes a chance on me again or be with the man I love?"

The man she loved. He wanted to hear that again.

"I wonder what is the soonest we can be married."

"I haven't said yes yet," she protested with a laugh.

"Don't you realize you've been saying yes for the last five minutes?" he refuted, taking her hands in his own. "I've heard yes."

"You're ridiculous," she said. But she stepped forward into his embrace.

"Yes," he agreed. Just as he'd agree to anything she said. Finally, he could hold her.

He closed the circle of his arms around her, burying his face against the silken skin of her cheek, her neck. What he had done before she had been there?

How had he ever breathed?

June 1816

Dear Cousin,

    I must tell you I am very upset. I shall never in my life ask for your advice again. It is exceedingly poor. My Georgie has married that woman and they are living in absolute squalor in the ruins of Auldale Castle. If it were not for your outrageous suggestion, I would not now be in this insufferable predicament. I feel very ill used and I shall not be visiting this fall.

        Mary Martin

June 1817

Dear Cousin,

    The child is a boy and shall be named George after his father and grandfather, whom he takes after. He definitely has the Martin nose.

As the nursery is not yet finished at the Castle, everyone is at the manor and what a delight it is to have John and my little Georgie living with me. The only benefit to having that woman as my daughter-in-law is that she listens to me, whereas John is still quite obstinate. At least they are happy with each other and John smiles and converses when we have company. I frequently remind them that if it were not for me knowing that Angelina would suit him, they would never have met.

Please do visit us as soon as you are able. Georgie is the finest of babies. Everyone who sees him is quite in awe.

Yours,

Mary

Want more?
Read on for a seductive excerpt of

ON THESE SILKEN SHEETS

by Sabrina Darby

CHAPTER ONE

Some things never change, Carolina thought as she pressed up against the wall of the library, obscured by shadows and long, voluminous draperies. She might be eighteen, in London, and at her first ball ever, but she was still stuck in the ignoble position of watching Henry Bosworth make love to another woman merely ten feet from where she hid.

He was older, of course. The mouth that now kissed the unknown woman's neck was that of a man and no longer a youth. And just as she had six years ago, watching his well-formed hands clutching a round bottom through layers of clothing, she imagined those hands on her.

A pause in the lady's moans drew Carolina's gaze upward. With a silent gasp, she flattened herself further against the unyielding wall.

Bosworth stared straight at her, a small smile curving his lips. Though the light in the room was dim, she knew his eyes would be green, that murky green that reminded her of marshes and ancient deities.

He murmured something to the woman in his arms and

the lady laughed, her bejeweled fingers *tsk*ing at him, even as she broke away. He followed her to the door, kissing her yet again, and then closed it behind her.

Carolina heard the faint but clear click of the lock.

Dear Lord, why had she decided to find a moment of privacy? That thought fled as she wondered if he would recognize her. She must look vastly different, all those awkward angles having given way to a fuller, more proportionate body.

She didn't, couldn't, move as Bosworth approached. She merely watched in appreciation, with baited breath, as this taller, more muscular version of him prowled across the room, peeling his gloves off as he came. His black hair glinted in the dim light. His breeches fit him as if molded to his frame, and she could see the distinct outline of his male part.

Would that part, too, have grown with age? she wondered, unconsciously licking her lips.

Now he was inches from her. She could smell him. She remembered that scent, of sandalwood and other spices—the sort of spices that permeated one's skin and lingered in one's mind long after the source was gone.

He extended one arm, resting his hand against the wall, close to her head. His other hand touched her cheek, one long finger running along her jaw.

She knew she should be frightened. She knew she should protest and run away, and indeed, she was terrified. Because his hand felt too good on her skin.

She stared at his sleeve, at the display of sartorial skill so close to her face.

"You like to watch," Bosworth stated, his voice low, gravelly, as if he had spent the last six years smoking cigars. And maybe he had. She knew nothing of him but that he'd been a friend of her father's back then—a guest stopping at their country house for the night.

She didn't answer, couldn't. But she dragged her eyes to his. She shivered as he trailed his finger down her neck, across the bare skin of her chest and finally dipped down into the ruffles of her dress, skimming the hollow between her breasts.

Abruptly his hand left her.

"I'd wager you're dripping wet," he murmured.

As if his words were magic, she felt the hot rush between her legs, the familiar aching heaviness.

In her single bed at night, it had always been him she had seen and imagined while her hands explored her body and brought her to ecstasy. In fact, the night six years ago that she had watched him between the downstairs maid's plump white thighs, arcing into her again and again, was the first night Carolina had thought about her own body that way— the first night her fingers had experimented.

His hand grasped her dress, lifting layers of cloth to bunch up between them. She opened her mouth to speak, to tell him to stop, but his bare hand was already above her stockings, on the naked flesh of her thigh, and moving upward.

He cupped her in his palm, his thumb brushing over the slight protrusion where all the sensations seemed to clump. Then he slid one long finger through the slick folds and entered her.

She moaned, her head turning toward his outstretched arm, even as her knees buckled.

His hand felt so much better than hers ever had.

"Molten velvet," Bosworth rasped, his hot, open mouth

meeting the tender flesh of her ear, nibbling, his tongue creating pinpoints of acute pleasure.

He started to withdraw the hand between her legs and suddenly Carolina found her voice.

"Wait, I'm almost there," she begged, feeling the tight spiral of pleasure nearing its peak.

He laughed against her.

"I like a woman who knows what she wants," he said, keeping his hand between her legs. His fingers stroked, working their magic until she finally exploded against him, shivering and bucking on his hand.

Henry shifted, reaching down to hold her up beneath her derriere. He hiked one of her silken legs around his waist and finally freed himself from the constraints of his breeches. The woman in his hands was still shivering with her own climax and his cock pulsed in empathy. He wanted nothing more in the world than to bury himself in her hot, wet depths.

His cock knew its way, unerringly finding the exquisitely yielding entrance. He thrust upward into her, reveling in the tightness.

God, she was small—a hot, wet glove stretching to fit him. The friction felt incredible. He groaned against her neck and grasped her buttocks with both hands. He pulled her down, even as he made a powerful thrust upward.

She cried out, stiffening against him in a way that had little to do with pleasure. For a moment, caught between the delicious feel of being buried to the hilt in her tight sheath and the shock of his discovery, he stilled.

"Please," she whispered, her breath ragged. He didn't know whether she begged him to stop or to continue.

He would never have guessed, never have imagined, that the stranger in his arms, who so passionately and willingly accepted his caresses in a library that belonged to neither of them, was a virgin.

Had been a virgin.

But that didn't matter anymore. What was done was done, and his body yearned for its own completion.

"It won't hurt the next time," he whispered, even as he retreated and then thrust again, following the instincts of his body. Letting go.

She smelled like honeysuckle, like lush, verdant summer, and he lost himself in the feel of her clenched around him. Tight as he thrust in. Tight and clinging as he pulled back and then sunk in once more. His mouth open in a guttural cry against her neck, he released himself inside her, his mind completely empty of anything but the overwhelming pleasure of the moment.

The storm passed. With a final shudder, Henry eased out of her body. He slowly released her leg and then took a half step back. She slumped against the wall, a look of shock on her face, and he laughed.

She might well be shocked. She'd just given a girl's most precious commodity to a stranger up against a wall.

"Who are you?" he wondered aloud. "No, wait," he said, when she parted her lips, "I don't want to know."

No, he thought, taking another step back. He would keep this as he had intended, a momentary affair. He had no wish for a wife, especially one he had only vetted sexually.

He looked down to button up the falls of his breeches, and even in the dim light, the reddish tint of her blood caught his eye. He extracted his handkerchief from its pocket and tidied himself up.

She hadn't moved. Still stood there, frozen.

He sighed and lifted her skirts once more. Her hand fluttered down to protest and he laughed again at that futile gesture.

There wasn't much blood on her thighs but what was there, he wiped away gently, unable to resist a few soft caresses, enjoying her shivering response.

"I recommend a trip to the retiring room to further clean yourself up," Henry suggested, dropping her skirts and coming to his feet.

The woman nodded but she still didn't move.

"I'll leave first," Henry said into the silence. "Wait a few and then you can follow."

The door closed behind him and Carolina finally shifted, her hand stealing down to the juncture of her thighs, pressing through the layers of cloth to the still pulsing mound. Inside, she was sore.

Henry Bosworth had just . . . had just had *relations* with her. And dear Lord, he didn't even know who she was!

Chapter Two

Henry stepped into the noise of the ballroom in a bit of a drunken stupor. Not that he'd had a drink, but he was fully sated and enjoying the post-coital languor. When he'd entered the library with Lady Islington, the assignation had been a bit of friendly flirtation—a momentary passion. He'd wanted a woman and that woman was willing.

But the lady he'd had instead—just thinking of the feel of her thighs in his hands stiffened his cock.

He almost turned around, thinking to stop her before she left the library, to have another go at her. But that was foolish. If he was caught with that erstwhile virgin he'd have to marry her. He'd done enough damage for one night.

What lovely damage.

The ballroom was cramped, crowded with people, many of whom he knew well. Since he'd inherited the title, most of them wanted to know him better.

The goddamned title.

As if reading the direction of his thoughts he heard a voice out of his past.

"Bosworth!" Nobody called him Bosworth anymore. Society much preferred Stanton, Viscount Stanton. It had taken Henry four years to get used to thinking of himself—not his older brother, James—as Stanton. James had been the viscount for most of Henry's life.

And now Henry was.

He swung around to meet the man who greeted him, recognizing him instantly. He hadn't seen Lord Hargreaves in four years. Not since Henry had retreated to his country seat to put his brother's affairs in order. Though Hargreaves was a good decade older, much of Henry's misspent youth had been in his company. In fact, his misspent youth was in a great part *due* to Hargreaves's influence.

"I haven't seen you in ages, boy!" Alistair Hargreaves appeared pleased to see him. The old satyr still looked strong and virile, despite his dissipation. His blond hair had started to turn gray, but only just. "But you're not Bosworth anymore. Congratulations on your inheritance."

Henry knew why Alistair congratulated him, because it meant Henry had money. When Henry had followed Alistair around London in the past, he had ridden the man's coattails. His own brother, James, had refused to finance his town life. Henry, himself, felt ambivalent about his brother's death.

"It's fortuitous to see you. I'm stuck attending these events for the season."

Henry arched an eyebrow up in inquiry but his eyes drifted toward the hallway door. He wanted another glimpse of the woman he'd fucked. He wanted to see what she looked like under the brighter lights of the illuminated ballroom.

"Did you ever meet my daughter, Carolina?"

Carolina. The name conjured up a vague image of a young girl, small for her age. He'd thought she was much younger than the twelve her father insisted on. And then, a memory he'd forced out of his mind from sheer embarrassment came crashing back.

Twenty-two and always randy, he'd been stopping with Alistair at the man's country house on the way to a house party. He'd plowed a receptive maid in the library, on a large leather-topped desk. Just as he released himself into her, arching back, he'd opened his eyes and looked up.

From the shadows of the carved wooden landing, the large, curious blue eyes of Alistair's twelve-year-old daughter looked down at him. She'd watched the whole episode.

Just like what had happened this evening. Eerily similar. A shiver of apprehension ran down Henry's back.

He nodded slowly.

"Well, she's eighteen now, so I had to bring her to London for her season. This is her first ball."

Henry heard the words, but he'd caught sight of a pale face under the archway. In the soft glow of the candlelight, she was even lovelier. He could also see just how young she was. Clearly not the experienced woman he'd first imagined.

Across the room, her eyes met his and widened. She grew even paler, and Henry felt the blood leave his own face.

Alistair followed his gaze.

"I see you recognize her." The baron's words chilled Henry's heart, confirming his worst suspicion. "She's grown up quite well. But she looks ill." An angry note entered Alistair's voice. "I do hope she isn't one of these frail girls. That won't do for marrying her off."

"She looks lovely, Hargreaves," Henry murmured, watching Carolina hesitantly approach them.

Something in Henry's voice must have alerted Alistair, because the baron glanced at him sharply.

"Stay away from her, Stanton," Alistair warned. "She's my daughter and an innocent."

"But of course," Henry agreed, laughing. And he thought once more of the feel of her wrapped around him, pulsing and wet.

Carolina reached them, a fluttering butterfly, her eyes darting from him to her father and then back to him. She'd managed to freshen her appearance and he imagined that only he would see the slight creases he'd created in her skirt when he'd bunched the fabric tightly in his hand.

"My dear, this is Lord Stanton." Henry watched surprise flicker in her blue eyes. "You've met before. Of course, he was merely Bosworth then."

"It is a delight to renew our acquaintance, Miss Hargreaves," Henry said, smiling and bowing over her hand.

"A pleasure," Carolina managed. "Father, I'm feeling a bit—"

"I would love nothing more than the pleasure of this dance," Henry cut her off, ignoring Alistair's frown and Carolina's slight shake of her head.

He didn't wait for an answer from either of them, just took her arm in his own and navigated her toward the dance floor.

"You *do* like to watch," he whispered, escorting her through the crowd.

He felt, more than saw, her flush.

"I didn't." Her protestation faltered as she took her place in the dance.

He saved his conversation for when the steps brought them close together.

"For the last twenty minutes, I've done nothing but think about you, about how it felt to thrust into you and feel you clench me tight."

They broke away again, and he had the benefit of seeing the effect his words had on her.

"I want you again."

CHAPTER THREE

Carolina was grateful that her governess had forced her to repeat the dance steps incessantly. If the moves had not been ingrained in her body, she was certain she would have stumbled and ruined the dance.

Bosworth's words resonated through her body.

"I want you again."

Hadn't he said it wouldn't hurt the next time? She wanted to know the pleasure. She shook her head slightly, trying to banish the thoughts. This was absolutely ridiculous. She'd already compromised herself completely and now she was thinking of continuing to act wantonly, disregarding all society's mores.

Who would want to marry her now?

That thought fled as quickly as it had come for she didn't really care. She knew that no matter what she wanted, she was only in town to be shown off, that her father would make the negotiations, pick a husband without any consultation.

And here, dancing with her, was the man who had captured her imagination all those years ago, who had actually possessed her just minutes ago.

She wanted him, too.

Six years ago, after he'd spotted her watching, he'd slid off the maid and dismissed the woman with a sensual pat on the rump. Carolina had looked curiously at the then much smaller manhood he hid away in his breeches. The mystery of the biology had fascinated her.

But then he'd hooked his finger and beckoned for her to come down and she had. There in the library, after the most fascinating visual lesson she'd ever had, in a room that smelled of sex, she got to know and fall in love with Henry Bosworth.

Stanton, she reminded herself firmly. She must call him Stanton now.

The dance ended.

He took her arm in his and even that slight contact made her dizzy.

"Meet me . . ."

He didn't finish his sentence. Her father had come forward to join them, his arm extended to take Carolina away.

"She looks a bit overwrought for her first night," Alistair said firmly. "But later I'll be at that club we used to frequent, if you're of the mind for it."

That club. More of a house of sin, where every hour of the night was an exercise in excess. Not a bad way to spend an evening, or a thousand evenings as Henry had. As Henry and Alistair had together.

He'd shared more women with the man than he could count. Now he'd had the man's daughter, too.

The baron had warned him off a good half hour too late.

138   SABRINA DARBY

Alistair should have hung a sign around the girl's neck proclaiming her identity.

Or maybe even that wouldn't have stopped Henry from stalking her across the room and ascertaining if indeed she was as aroused by watching as he'd guessed.

He studied their figures disappearing into the crowd in the direction of the entryway. Carolina's skirt swayed with each step, clinging ever so subtly now to the left side of her derriere and now to the right. Henry was as hard as a rock.

He thought briefly about finding Lady Islington and finishing off where they had started. *No.* The club would do well enough.

ABOUT THE AUTHOR

SABRINA DARBY has been reading romance since the age of seven and learned her best vocabulary (dulcet, diaphanous, and turgid) from them. She started writing romance the day after her wedding when she woke up with an idea for a Regency; she's been back in the early nineteenth century ever since. She can be found online at TheBallroomBlog.com, SabrinaDarby.com and Twitter.com/SabrinaDarby.

Give in to your impulses . . .
Read on for a sneak peek at four brand-new
e-book original tales of romance
from Avon Books.
Available now wherever e-books are sold.

CIRCLE OF DANGER
By Carla Swafford

HEAT RISES
By Alice Gaines

SOMEBODY LIKE YOU
By Candis Terry

A MOST NAKED SOLUTION
By Anna Randol

An Excerpt from

CIRCLE OF DANGER

by Carla Swafford

The top-secret assassins of The Circle are back and on the hunt for a dangerous drug lord capable of bringing women to the brink of pleasure . . . and devastation.

Marie Beltane, a lowly data-entry specialist intent on proving she's worthy of being a full operative, has just been injected with the drug responsible for the death of four local women . . . a drug that puts her sex drive into overdrive.

Arthur Ryker wants nothing more than to protect Marie, even if it means fulfilling her drug-induced . . . needs. But now a new evil has reared its ugly head—how far is Arthur willing to go to find an antidote and save the woman he always loved?

AN AVON RED NOVEL

CHAPTER ONE

Arthur Ryker sprang out of bed and immediately stood at attention, feet apart, his scarred hands in the "ready" position at waist level. One hand cupped by the other, restrained but prepared to kill. He shook his head and sighed. Just once he wanted to leave his bed like a regular person and not like a trained monkey.

"A bad dream?" a deep voice asked from the bedroom entrance. With one pierced black eyebrow lifted, Jack Drago leaned against the doorjamb.

Ignoring the question, Ryker walked naked into the bathroom. When he returned to grab some clothes out of the closet, Jack hadn't moved, but his gaze had most likely inspected every inch of the room. There wasn't much to see. A king-sized bed sat in a corner while a mirrorless dresser was centered against one wall—no pictures or the usual bric-a-brac to give away the occupant's personality. Then again, maybe it did. Rather stark for a man who owned enough properties and businesses to keep his organization in the best covert weapons money could buy. He didn't care what Jack thought about his bedroom. Except for a few hours of sleep and a shower and shave, Ryker rarely spent time in the room.

"What do you want?" he asked, glaring at his second-in-command.

With cold blue eyes, Jack studied him, then his gaze shifted away.

Ryker grunted. Not many people could deal with looking at the thick scars down the side of his body, but it was his blind eye that bothered most. White from the scar tissue damaged in a fire so many years ago, it was normally hidden beneath a patch. But Ryker'd be damned before he slept with one on. So if Jack decided to make a habit of waking him in the morning, he could fucking well get use to the sight. Considering the man had four visible piercings—and who knew how many hidden—along with tattoos covering one arm, Jack shouldn't have a problem with his scars. The man understood pain.

With sure, quick movements, he thrust his legs into jeans and yanked on a black T-shirt. After tugging on his boots, he strapped a small pistol at his ankle. With his patch in place, using his fingers he combed hair over the strap securing its position. Hell, he needed a haircut again. Maybe he'd shave his head like Jack. A simple enough solution. If only the rest of his problems could be so easily solved.

"She's in trouble," Jack said in an even tone as if his voice could defuse a bad situation.

Ryker's stomach and chest tightened as if he'd been hit. He knew who Jack referred to without adding a name. She happened to be part of why his life was so complicated.

"Did you hear me?" Jack straightened his stance.

"Yeah." Desire to break someone's neck raced through his body. "Where is she? What happened?"

With a sharp snap, he inserted a snub-nose into the shoulder holster hanging at his side and jerked on his leather jacket. He gritted his teeth for a few seconds to regain his composure. Then he took a deep breath, squared his shoulders, and exhaled.

"Last time Bryan heard from her, she'd entered the target's house in Chattanooga and was downloading information off a laptop. He lost communication with her." Jack quickly stepped out of the way for Ryker to move into the dark hallway. "They believe she's still in the house. If the Wizard sticks to his MO, we'll have about three hours before he takes her away or kills her."

Ryker wasted no time in reaching a massive room with mirrors from ceiling to floor. When the mansion was built in the eighteen hundreds, the room was used as a ballroom. It was empty now, except for a Steinway covered with a white sheet, and the high-sheen hardwood floor sounded hollow as he tramped across it. He used the room for one purpose only—to reach the stairwell hidden behind one of the mirrors.

"Took you long enough to spit it out." Ryker glanced at his second-in-command.

Jack remained quiet, staring straight ahead. Ryker didn't really expect an excuse. The man knew how he felt about that. No excuse for failure, especially when it came to protecting Marie.

Four months earlier, Ryker had moved The Circle compound from the suburbs of Atlanta to an area near the Smoky

Mountains. The mansion was situated in the middle of almost ten thousand acres, which included a large mountain filled with a network of tunnels and bunkers perfect to house the facility he needed. Last year, the final phase of the project was completed and now they were training new recruits in the underground Sector. The nearly fifteen square miles provided the privacy he needed. In a world filled with evil people, his covert organization of assassins came in handy.

Their footsteps echoed in the long, well-lit tunnel. A semi could pass through the passageway without scraping the side mirrors or the tips of muffler stacks.

"Who was her backup?" Ryker asked.

When a few seconds passed without an answer, Ryker stopped and faced Jack.

"They're handling it."

Ryker continued to stare.

His second-in-command sighed. "She went in without a backup."

Jaw clenched, Ryker strode to the iris scan next to a large metal door. A buzz sounded and he slammed the door against the inner wall.

The gripping pain in his belly grew and reminded him of the fear he had lived with for years before he took over control of The Circle. She could not keep doing this to him. He refused to allow anything more to happen to her. She knew this and still didn't listen.

The noise level in the basketball court-sized room almost broke the sound barrier with printers running and people shouting or talking to those sitting next to them—or to others on the Internet or satellite phones—along with the clicking of keyboards. Each wall covered with large screens captured a different scene of people living their lives in various parts of the world. In the center of the room, faces bleached white by the monitors in front of them, the supervisors and handlers communicated with their operatives.

Ryker stopped in the middle of the bullpen, searching for his prey.

The balding, whipcord-thin Bryan Tilton stood over a handler shouting instructions and pointing at the screen. Maybe a sixth sense alerted Bryan. He looked up and his eyes widened.

Ryker charged toward him, ignoring the people ducking for cover behind partitions and beneath desks.

"You son of a bitch!"

His fist clipped Bryan on the chin, sending the man sliding across the floor. Desire to flatten the asshole's pointy nose almost overrode all of Ryker's control. Good thing Bryan remained sprawled out on the linoleum.

Standing over the man, Ryker opened and closed his fists. The temptation to punish him further for his stupidity warred with the fear of jabbing the cartilage of the idiot's nose into his brain.

"I swear, sir, I told her to wait until I could get backup in place, but she wouldn't listen." Bryan cupped his jaw and shifted it from side to side. "Two of our operatives are held up in a traffic accident about twenty-five miles from her last location."

"Last location?" Ryker gritted his teeth.

"The target's house, off Riverview Road." Bryan scooted back when Ryker took a step. The man's head bobbled on his skinny neck. "As soon as Phil and Harry reach it, they'll extract her."

Afraid he would crack the man's chicken neck, Ryker turned away and pointed at the nearest handler. "You! Sal?"

Mohawk trembling, the pale man nodded.

Ryker said, "Tell Phil and Harry to call me on my cell as soon as they reach the house. Do not go inside! Jack and I will be there in twenty minutes. Have them wait for us. AHH" He turned back to Bryan. "Have the Spirit ready in five minutes." His helicopter could cover the miles quickly and land almost anywhere.

Marie Beltane struggled against the chains restraining her on a cot that reeked of sex and urine. She stifled a groan. No, no, no. Nausea traveled up her throat.

All the beams and pipes overhead felt like they were squeezing the air out of the room. Basements were never among her favorite rooms. The dampness and creepy-crawly things always gave her the willies.

She still couldn't believe she'd been caught. Bryan had sworn it would be an easy gig. Prior surveillance had revealed the man worked each evening at a massive bank of computers. Go in and download a flash drive load of info and get out. The target always left his house at nine in the morning and didn't return until nine that evening. Breaking into the house when most people ate dinner in the surrounding homes had sounded so easy. Few would look out their windows as they settled down in front of their plates or televisions or both.

Hours would pass before he returned home. But he came back early.

Oh, God, she'd screwed up big time!

He looked like a fourteen-year-old with his cartoon-themed T-shirt and his mop of hair, but she knew from his file he was between twenty-six and twenty-eight. During their surveillance, they never got a clear photograph of him. Whenever he entered or exited his house, he did so through his garage. His SUV had tinted windows, preventing anyone from seeing inside.

The man standing with his back to her had outmaneuvered every defensive tactic she'd been taught. He didn't fight like a kid. Jack was right. She needed to work harder on her moves. If she had, she wouldn't be in this predicament. The nerd had surprised her, taking her down with unexpected ease.

She refused to cry even though she couldn't stop the trembling in her body. Every inch ached from his battery of hits and kicks. For a scrawny man, he'd moved fast and hit hard.

Her head hurt from holding back tears. She'd hoped never to be in this position again, to be under someone's control. No matter how many times she reminded herself this was different from before, the horror of repeating history pushed her to keep her eyes open. Staying aware of her enemy helped to keep her calm.

"You're not very smart. I'm efficient in seven different types of martial arts." His stiff words failed to impress her. He moved, revealing what he held in his hand. The huge syringe with a shiny green substance in the barrel had a needle longer than her forefinger. "Just because I'm a geek doesn't mean I'm unacquainted with ways to defend myself."

Marie stared at the needle. The duct tape covering her mouth muffled her scream. Ever since he jumped her, she'd tried to see a way to escape, while keeping calm.

She tried to be brave. She kept telling herself that screaming would only be a waste of energy. Stifling the panic engulfing her would keep her alive.

"Wait until this stuff hits your bloodstream. I'm told the sensation is similar to that last second before reaching an orgasm. In other words, you'll do anything to get off." He chuckled and lifted her shirt. He tugged at the waistband of her jeans.

She flinched when the needle slid into the soft skin near her hip.

"Perfect for where I'm sending you." He jerked on the jeans until the tips of his fingers brushed her pubic hair. "White American women—especially petite, natural blondes like you—are quite popular in parts of the Middle East and Asia. Virgins are preferred but rare here unless we go much younger." He shrugged. "Then you get into Amber Alerts and they're too much trouble. Anyway, bitches like you are plentiful and disposable."

He pulled harder at her jeans, taking her panties down.

She froze. Her stomached churned with the thought of what he might do next. Then he pushed the needle deeper. The liquid burned, becoming hotter as he eased the plunger down. The pain took her mind off her fear for only a second. When she tried to move away, the rattling chains reminded her she wasn't going anywhere. Tears pooled at the corner of her eyes and she turned her head, refusing to let him see her cry.

"A formula created by . . . a fucking genius! Especially created to use on sneaky sluts like you. The Wizard is a god!" He laughed. The back of his hand grazed her cheek. "I know it stings, baby. Sorry . . . no. I'm not sorry. You have the look of an ice princess. I love seeing an uptight cunt like you suffer. You have no idea what you've gotten yourself into. This wonder drug is highly addictive and from what I'm told, it has long-lasting effects. You'll grow to love it."

The grin on his smooth face terrified her more than anything else he'd done. Her vision blurred. The man leaned over her, his brown eyes dark and merciless. She whimpered. Every cell of her body tingled.

"Do you feel it? It takes a little while to set in. The Wizard said it tingles all over and next, for a small time, you'll feel like you're floating on water. Then you'll get sleepy and then— *bam!*—you'll be like a bitch in heat." He cackled and thrust his groin several times against her leg and the side of the cot. He punched the air with his fist and did a little dance. When he turned his back, he reached for something on a table nearby. "Now let's see what all of you looks like."

Light glinted off the scalpel. He swiped at the air above her as if he wielded a sword. No matter how brave she tried to be earlier, she couldn't stop her limbs from shaking harder and her stomach from twisting. She squealed behind the tape.

The sound of slicing material had her arching away from his touch. *Please don't cut me. Oh, please, God, help.* In seconds, he peeled away her clothes. He rubbed his groin and a lascivious grin marred his youthful face.

"Not bad, though I find the scars a shame, yet rather interesting. It looks like someone used a belt or whip on you.

Have you been a bad girl?" He slid his hand down her bare thigh and over a long, thin white scar. "There are clients who would love to add to them."

She turned her head. Swallowing several times to keep from choking on vomit, she concentrated on the number of blocks in the basement wall. She could get through this. It wouldn't be the first time her body had been used. Eventually, she'd find a way out.

Just as she heard his zipper go down, a loud blast shook the walls. Dust sprinkled onto her face. She blinked her eyes. The room looked smoky, choked with plaster powder.

"What the hell?" The man ran toward the stairs as he struggled to pull up his pants. One foot on the bottom step, he stopped, staring at the door.

A smaller blast was followed by shouting and heavy footsteps running across the floor above. Whoever had come a-knocking were making their way through the house.

"Well, babe, you're on your own. I hope they appreciate the gift I'm leaving them." He laughed and disappeared beneath the stairs into a black void.

Her eyelids felt so heavy. Tingling traveling across her torso rushed down her legs and arms, and then a feeling of lightness and floating followed. A strong breeze brushed her naked body. Someone had found the basement. A wave of dizziness pushed her under and she closed her eyes, unable to lift them even when she felt someone fighting with the chains holding her down.

"Damn it, Marie. You'd better be alive," a deep voice growled.

She smiled. Deep inside, she knew he'd come for her.

An Excerpt from

HEAT RISES
by *Alice Gaines*

Welcome to Alice Gaines's "Cabin Fever" series: Who knows what naughty games you'll play when you've got nowhere else to go? Laura Barber gets to put her imagination to the test when she finds herself snowbound in a cabin with Ethan Gould, a man she's dreamt of doing unspeakably delicious things to for years. Find out what happens when . . . *Heat Rises.*

AN AVON RED NOVELLA

CHAPTER ONE

So much for making it to her job interview. Laura Barber might as well have been looking at a moonscape rather than a deserted mountain highway. Still shivering, she gazed out the window of the country store as the falling snow covered the pavement and filled in the road completely. The storm had started only half an hour ago. What would this place look like by morning?

"You're a mighty lucky young lady," said the shopkeeper, handing her a Styrofoam cup with steam coming out the top. "If you'd gone off the road any farther from here, you'd still be out in that."

She took a sip of the coffee and did her best not to grimace at the bitter taste. The man may be right about her luck, but she'd probably ruined her shoes on the trek here. The low-heeled pumps had cost a bundle, and she'd worn them just enough that her feet felt comfortable when she dressed for business.

"Yep," the man said as he gazed out at the accumulating snow. "Nobody'll be moving around in these parts for days."

"Mister—"

"Beaumont," he said, offering his gnarled hand.

"Mr. Beaumont," she said, studying him as they shook hands. The twinkle in his blue eyes suggested more youth than the fringe of white hair did. If you called central casting for a country store owner, they'd probably send someone like this man.

"You'd be in a heap of trouble if you'd broken down farther away," he said.

"Can someone come out and put me back on the road before things get worse?" she asked.

"You don't understand storms in these mountains, Miss."

"Ms.," she said. "Ms. Laura Barber."

"Well, Ms. Barber, won't nobody get out of here until the plows come through."

"When will that be?"

"Days," he answered. "Probably not a week, though."

"A week?" Darn it all. She was supposed to be at the bottom of this mountain by evening and at an interview in the morning. She'd planned carefully to get ahead of this storm, but her plane had landed late. Still, she ought to have been able to make her destination. She'd grown up in Connecticut and had driven in winter weather before. Snow was snow, wasn't it? Apparently not.

"What am I going to do?" she asked. "I can't stay here for days."

"That you can't. I'll be closing up and heading home in a few minutes."

"Is there a motel nearby?" she asked.

"Nope. We'll have to find a family to put you up."

"I can't impose on strangers for days."

He shrugged. "Don't see that you have much choice."

Wonderful. Not only would she not make it to her interview but she'd also have to spend days with people she didn't know. She managed well enough in business situations where procedures and rules of engagement were clearly laid out. In someone's home, she'd have to interact. She probably couldn't disappear behind her laptop without appearing rude.

"Unless . . ." Mr. Beaumont said. "Your solution might be pulling up right now."

Headlights shone in from outside—bright enough to blind her for a moment—a huge SUV or pickup, with its engine at a low roar. The motor shut off, and the lights went dim. A man climbed out and headed into the store. A blast of cold air whooshed in through the front as he entered. "Hey, Phil."

Mr. Beaumont shuffled off. "Hey, you young pup. What are you doing out in weather like this?"

"Business down in the city. Thought I could outrun the storm."

The voice tugged at her memory. Low and dark. She knew it. Even though she hadn't heard it recently enough to place it in her brain, something about the tone registered in her body.

She glanced over at the counter where he stood, his back to her. Tall and broad-shouldered, he commanded the space around him. She had a physical memory of that too, enough to warm her skin. Whoever this was, she'd do best to avoid him. But how?

"Good thing you're here," Mr. Beaumont said, gesturing toward her. "This lady is going to need a ride somewhere."

The man turned and all the memory nudges turned into one huge sucker punch. Ethan Gould.

Good Lord, not him. It had to be five years . . . no, six. That night at the party. After three years of fantasies about the handsome guy who always sat at the front of the class, she'd decided to at least try to find out if the attraction was mutual. Tequila fortification, too much, had led to a night of humiliation. Oh God, all the things she'd said to him. Her stomach sank remembering them after all this time.

Other than that, they'd almost never interacted all through business school. He'd have forgotten her by now. Women probably came on to him all the time—women more remarkable than herself. He wouldn't remember. Please God, don't let him remember.

Sure enough, he smiled at her as he would at any stranger. A genial expression he used so easily. The famed Gould charm would come next. So potent it worked even on men. On women . . . well, forget trying to resist it.

After a moment, his brows knitted together. "Do we know each other?"

"No . . . I don't think . . . haven't met," she said. Damn it all, how could he force this reaction from her after so much time? She'd actually lie about her identity if she could get away with it. She'd avoided him successfully since that horrible night. She'd actually followed his career so that she'd know where he was. He couldn't have just happened on her on a snowy mountain, and yet here he stood, as tempting and as terrifying as he'd been at that party.

"This is Ms. Laura Barber," Mr. Beaumont said. "You two know each other?"

"Right." Recognition dawned in his amber eyes, followed by a slight tension to his jaw. Remembering, no doubt. Her skin went from warm to burning. By now, her face would be a bright pink.

He recovered quickly, with a big smile. He still had perfect teeth, of course, and perfect skin. Only his too-large ears kept him from total perfection, but the flaw made him all the more attractive.

"It's been a while," he said. "Good to see you again."

"Hi." A stupid reply but innocent enough, she thought.

"Seeing as you two know each other, won't you mind taking Ms. Barber to where she wants to go?" Mr. Beaumont asked.

He rested a hand on a nearby rack of magazines and struck a casual pose. A light of cunning in his eyes belied his apparent ease. "Where are you headed?"

"The city," she said. "I'm already late."

"How'd you get this far?"

"Rental car"—she gestured toward the outside as if she could point at the thing—"I ran off the road."

"Can't say I'm surprised," he said, his gaze never leaving her face. She did her best to look straight back at him, but she'd never win a staring contest with this man. Eventually, she gave up and studied his shoes, instead. Boots, rather—the sort ranchers wore. His had a broken-in appearance, as did the faded jeans that covered his legs up to the hem of his shearling jacket.

"We won't be getting to the city tonight," he said. "But we can make it to my friend's cabin."

"Cabin?" she repeated. "In the middle of a blizzard?"

"My friend's an engineer. The place is self-sufficient with a generator and solar panels."

"The sun's not out now," she said. In fact, with the heavy snow, it was already dark.

"And storage batteries," he said. "We'll be fine."

"I haven't agreed to go with you."

"What choice do you have?" he asked, as he straightened and pulled a slip of paper from his jacket. "I'll need a few things, Phil."

"Coming right up." Mr. Beaumont took the list from him and retreated to the back of the store.

"Look, this is really nice of you—"

Before she could get the "but" out, he took a step toward her. " 'Nice' isn't exactly the word I was thinking of."

She made herself stand her ground, even though everything in her wanted to back away. "I don't want to impose."

"Don't be silly. No one around here would put someone out on a night like this."

"Mr. Beaumont said he'd find a family here to take me in."

He crossed his arms over his chest. "So, you're a social butterfly now? Happy to move in with strangers for several days?"

Damn him, he knew she wasn't. He had to remember from graduate school that she kept to herself, quietly getting top grades from her place in the back of the class.

"I . . . I . . ." Damn it. He actually had her stuttering. She took a breath. "I can't go with you."

"Why not?" he asked, as he studied her, his gaze assessing and not without a light of admiration. Her heartbeat responded, speeding up. The feeling might be pleasant with another man—one who hadn't heard about her sexual fantasies after she'd had too many margaritas. She'd told him about how her mind had wandered during boring lectures, imagining how his hands would feel on her breasts. About how she played images of him in her mind when she used her vibrator. She'd even asked if his sex was as big as she'd imagined it, and then giggled when she'd fumbled against his pants and discovered it was even larger. Oh God, humiliation. Utter and total humiliation.

"Maybe you're afraid to be alone with me," he said. He might have read her mind.

"Ridiculous." Okay, that was a lie, but she wouldn't cower before him. She'd gone on from that night to establish a good career. As a grown woman with more experience since graduate school, she shouldn't have to fear men any longer, even this one. Even if she did, she wouldn't let him know he frightened her.

"Laura, you have a choice of crowding in with a family you don't know or sharing a cabin with me. I won't even speak to you if you don't want."

"I don't think that will be necessary." Great. She'd agreed to go with him. No matter. A few days together, and she'd get away again.

"Good." He smiled yet again, the blasted man. "The cabin it is."

Y**ou** could have knocked Ethan Gould over with a feather. First, to run into Laura Barber at Phil Beaumont's store, way out here in the middle of no place. At least there was a logical explanation for that. She was probably up for the same job at Henderson that he was. A bit odd, as their talents—skill sets, she would have called them—lay in very different areas. But they were both übercompetent, as any headhunter would have to know. Still, what were the chances that she'd end up at that country store, needing a ride in one of the mountains' worst storms of the season just as he pulled in? Fate was trying to tell them something, and he, for one, was listening.

The fact that she'd end up staying with him in an isolated cabin fell into a different category of unlikelihood. Impossibility, more like. And yet, there she sat in the bucket seat next to his, staring out at the snow as if it held some message.

Laura Barber, the shy thing who'd turned into a wild woman one night, nearly dragging him into an empty bedroom at the end-of-semester party. The woman who'd promised sex so uninhibitedly she'd singed the edges of his imagination. The woman who never spoke up in class but who'd whispered filthy words in his ear while she'd unfastened his belt and started in on the zipper of his slacks. Unfortunately, she'd given off enough clues of her intoxicated state to keep him from following through, just barely managing to stop things before they'd gone too far.

Laura Barber . . . the one who got away. Hell, the one he'd let get away. Damn his conscience all to hell.

"Do you own this truck?" she asked after several minutes of silence.

"Rented."

"Do you always drive something so big?"

Right. The queen of green. "What were you driving?"

"A hybrid."

"If you'd had one of these, you wouldn't have gone off the road."

"Touché." She looked him in the eyes for probably the first time since she'd climbed aboard. "Truce?"

"Sure." Although, how he'd manage that would take some mental gymnastics. She wore the same scent she had all through business school. Nothing exotic, just kind of clean and sweet. She'd wrapped the scent around him that night. It still went straight to his gut, and now he had the mother of all hard-ons. Truce, indeed.

He stared out the windshield. "That your hybrid up ahead?"

She squinted, peering forward. "It is."

He pulled up beside the car, set the brake, and pushed the gear lever to park. "Leave the engine running for heat. Give me your keys."

"I can get my bag myself."

He held out his hand. "I thought we had a truce."

After fishing in her purse, she produced a key on rental company chain and handed it over. Now, he could get away from her perfume for a few seconds. Maybe the cold would do something to ease his boner too.

He climbed out of the truck and shut the door behind him. His boots sinking into snow halfway to his knees, he trudged the few feet to the hybrid and used the key to open the trunk. She traveled light—just one carry-on and a suit bag. If he looked inside, which he wouldn't, he'd no doubt find a formless skirt and jacket combination. She could almost, but not quite, hide her plush figure under all the layers of clothing she wore.

After closing the trunk, he scrambled back to the truck and stowed her things in the back. Then he took his seat in front and set the gear to low to take them down the frosted highway.

"You seem to know your way around," she said.

"I grew up near here."

"You look the part. All you need is a Stetson." She actually smiled. Not much but enough to curve that tempting lower lip. No matter how hard she tried to blend into the woodwork, that mouth and her enormous brown eyes kept her from pulling it off. Great, now he was thinking about her mouth.

"What are you doing in these parts?" he asked, even though he had a pretty good idea of the answer.

"Job interview," she answered.

"Henderson?"

"How did you know?"

"My interview is day after tomorrow," he said. "Doesn't look as if either of us is going to make it."

She groaned. "Oh no."

"Don't worry. You still have a chance."

"Why wouldn't I?" she said. "They'll understand about the storm."

"I didn't mean that. I meant the competition."

"What . . . oh." She glared at him. "You don't think I can beat you for the job."

He didn't answer but only smiled.

"Competitive to the end, eh?" she said.

"Pot . . . kettle."

"Is this your idea of a truce?"

"Sorry. Force of habit." He turned the truck off the main highway onto the narrow road that led to Jeff's cabin. Here, even the four-wheel drive wouldn't help them if he made a bad move. He'd have to concentrate on something besides the chaos in his jeans. The heavy vehicle inched along while the wipers slap-slapped against the windshield and the wind howled outside, swirling the snow around them. Laura sat huddled in the corner, her arms wrapped around her ribs.

"Frightened?" he asked.

She bit her lower lip. Even a short glimpse of that out of the corner of his eye put his mind in places where it didn't belong.

"A little," she said after a moment.

"I'll take care of you." Boy, howdy, would he. *Stop it, damn it. Now.*

Normally, she'd have bristled at any suggestion that she needed help with anything. She must have been really scared not to say a word but just sit there, making herself small. If he wasn't careful, she'd start tugging at his protective instincts. But then, when had he ever been careful where a woman was concerned? Well, maybe once . . . with this woman.

"Is it much farther?" she asked.

"A few more yards." Of course, in a storm in the mountains, a few more yards could stretch on forever. How had the pioneers ever managed?

The cabin came up on him unexpectedly. He must have misjudged how far they'd come because the outline of the building appeared directly ahead of them before he'd realized they'd arrived. He let a breath out slowly, and his shoulders relaxed. Though he'd never admit it to Laura, navigating under these conditions was a bit of a crapshoot, and he hadn't felt all that comfortable himself.

He steered the truck into the carport and cut the engine. When he turned off the headlights, they fell into darkness for a moment. All the better for him to sense the woman next to him. Her scent and the sound of her breathing filled the space around him. It was going to be an interesting few days.

If the cabin had appeared rustic from the outside, the interior somehow managed romantic and high-tech at the same time. Laura left her ruined shoes in the enclosed entryway, what Ethan referred to as a "mini mudroom," and followed him into the main living area. When he hit the switch, lights came on around the baseboards, producing enough illumination to suggest the interior of an elegant restaurant.

"Solar power?" she asked as she tipped up her carry-on and draped the suit bag over it.

"From batteries beneath the house," he said. "The system gives off heat as well as light."

"And the heat rises to fill the room."

"Once I get the woodstove and a fire going, we'll be toasty."

"Nice." They'd been bandying that word around a lot. This time, it didn't carry extra meaning.

Ethan put the bag of groceries on the counter in the kitchenette. "Settle in."

She glanced around. "Are there other rooms?"

"Bathroom."

"Then, where would you like me to settle in?"

He paused in the act of stowing a carton of eggs in the refrigerator. After a moment, he straightened, placed his elbow on the door and assumed his too-casual pose again. "You take the sleeping loft. I'll camp out on the couch."

She checked the piece of furniture in question. "Is it big enough for you?"

"I'll fold into it."

"Because, I don't really have to—"

"Take the loft. As you observed, heat rises. You'll be comfortable up there."

The baseboard heating was having an effect on the temperature, but not enough for her to remove her coat.

"I'll lay a fire," she said.

"You know how to do that?"

"It's not rocket science."

"Be my guest."

While he continued putting away groceries, she went to the huge stone fireplace and knelt to check out the supplies. Plenty of wood and kindling. Starting with crumpled newspaper, she built what should soon be a good blaze. She found matches, lit the paper, and sat back on her heels to watch the fuel catch.

Out of nowhere, a male hand appeared in front of her, holding a glass of red wine. She took it and glanced up at the towering figure of Ethan Gould. "Thanks."

"I didn't know for sure if you'd want anything to drink."

"I'm good with wine. It's tequila I need to stay away from." Damn it, why had she said that? She shouldn't have mentioned anything that could remind him of that night. Or remind herself, for that matter. She sipped some of her drink and stared into the fire.

Of course, he didn't do the easy thing and go back to the kitchenette and leave her alone with the memory. Oh no, he had to sit down beside her in front of the fire.

"Want to talk about the two-ton elephant in the room?" he asked.

"No."

"I do."

"Fine," she said. "You talk. I'll listen."

"Doesn't work that way."

"Look, Ethan." She took a fortifying sip of her wine and let it roll around on her tongue. He had good taste, she'd give him that. Eventually, she had to face him. When she did, she somehow ended up lost in the reflection of the fire in his eyes.

"Laura . . ." he prompted.

"I wasn't myself that night." Lord, how embarrassing. If he wanted to talk about this, why didn't he say something or do something? Why was he putting it all on her? "I behaved inappropriately toward you."

He gave her a lopsided smile. "Is that what they're calling it now?"

"Please. You'll make me blush."

"So what?" he said. "No one's ever died of blushing."

She could. Her heart fluttered in her chest, and her stomach felt full of cold lead. When her hands trembled, she set her glass on the hearth rather than spill red wine on the carpet.

"Hey, hey." He put his glass next to hers and took her hands in his. "It's not that serious."

When she couldn't take any more gazing into his eyes, she

switched to staring at the fire. "You could probably have sued me for harassment."

"Harassment?" he repeated. "How do you figure that?"

"You obviously didn't welcome . . . um, feel the same . . ."

"Because I didn't follow through?"

She clenched her teeth together and sat in utter, silent shame.

"You'd had too much to drink, Laura," he said. "Only a bastard takes advantage like that."

"Well," she pulled her hands from his and took a steadying breath. "It was a long time ago. I'm glad we settled it."

"I don't call that settled," he said.

She stared into the fire again. If she didn't look at him, maybe he'd go away. "I do."

"Damn it, Laura, you're going to deal with this." Taking her chin in his hand, he turned her head until she had to look at him. "Do you know how exciting you were that night?"

"I was drunk and disorderly." Drunk enough for him to have rejected her but not enough for her to have forgotten all the things she'd said to him. No one on earth had ever heard of her fantasies, but after that encounter, this man had.

"You turned me on like crazy," he said. "I went nuts trying to figure out how to get you to make the same invitation sober."

"It was a long time ago, Ethan."

"I would have called you, but I figured that would have embarrassed you."

"I'm glad you didn't."

"I kept putting myself in places where I'd bump into you

by accident, but you disappeared"—he gestured with both hands—"poof."

"I don't want to talk about this," she said. "You promised."

He studied her for a long moment before picking up his wine again. "Yeah, I guess I did."

"Thanks for understanding." This time, when she lifted her glass, it didn't wobble.

"You'll at least eat dinner with me, I hope."

"Of course," she said. "This is excellent wine, by the way."

"It should go with the steaks. How do you like yours?"

"Rare."

"Rare it is." With the knuckle of his free hand, he tapped the end of her nose before rising and sauntering back to the stove.

She took a deep breath—the first truly relaxing one she'd had since he strolled into the country store—and watched him rinse vegetables for salad in the sink. She ought to help him, but he seemed to know what he was about. Besides, the world was a safer place with distance between them.

So, he'd refused her that night out of gallantry. Or so he said. That made things marginally less humiliating. Sort of.

As he worked on their dinner, his movement fluid as he went from counter to refrigerator to cabinet and back, she couldn't erase the memory of that lean body against hers. The kisses . . . sweeter and more potent than the margaritas that had caused her to lose control. And the misery, the soul-crushing disappointment, when he'd pushed her away.

Now that they'd discussed the two-ton elephant, the whole incident was closed. Over and dealt with. Finito. Somehow, that only made her stomach sink even lower.

An Excerpt from

SOMEBODY LIKE YOU

by *Candis Terry*

Welcome Back to the Sugar Shack

Straitlaced . . . Chicago prosecutor Kelly Silverthorne has a perfect record in the courtroom and a big fat zero in the bedroom. When she loses her first case ever, she returns home to Deer Lick, Montana, to regain her confidence and shake off the "Sister Serious" moniker she's been strapped with since childhood. Only a few hours into her repentance, karma thrusts her face-to-face with yet another of her major fiascos—a one-night stand with the hottest cop in the county.

Rebel with a Cause . . . Deputy James Harley has always played with fire. When smart and sexy Kelly pops back into his life, he doesn't mind going for a full burn. And that might be exactly what happens when his past threatens to catch up with his future.

A Match Made in . . . Heaven only knows what Kelly's dearly departed mom has planned from the *other side*—especially since she's already meddled in Kelly's siblings' love lives. But even heaven knows that when love comes knocking, there's no stopping the good things to come.

CHAPTER ONE

Kelly Silverthorne despised killers.

Especially the type who possessed the charm of a movie star that belied the icy heart of the snake that beat in their chest.

"I think it's dead."

Jarred from the dark images in her head, Kelly looked up at her fellow Chicago prosecutor, Daniel Bluhm. A streak of sunlight shot through the window of the deli and glimmered in his golden hair. While they awaited word that the jury had reached a verdict in the Colson murder case, lunch had seemed a good idea. The nerves coiled in her stomach said otherwise. "Excuse me?"

"Your potato salad." Daniel pointed to her plate. "Or maybe I should call it lumpy soup."

Kelly glanced down at the fork in her hand and the mess she'd made of what had once been a tasty side dish. She dropped the utensil to her plate and glanced around the old-fashioned restaurant and the retro decorations that adorned the walls. "Sorry."

A smile crossed his mouth before he stuffed in the last bite of his patty melt. "Nervous?"

She nodded.

"You did a hell of a job with closing arguments."

"Daniel?" Kelly sipped her diet Pepsi and wiped her mouth with the paper napkin. "I don't know if I mentioned this or not, but this murder case we've been working on for more than a year? The case in which I pushed for an arrest and prosecution against the state attorney's better judgment? The case I swore we had enough evidence to get a conviction?"

"You mean the case that's been plastered all over the real *and* entertainment news networks?"

"Yes!" Her eyes widened in feigned surprise and she pointed at him with the straw in her soda. "*That* one. In case I forgot to tell you, it involves a popular movie-starlike senator and a glamorous cast member of "Real Housewives of Chicago." By the time I wrapped up, the jury looked at me like I'd kicked their dog."

"Don't be so hard on yourself." Her partner chuckled. "We went in prepared. We had forensics, motive, and—"

"No body." She shrugged. "Bottom line, Bluhm. No. Body." Kelly grabbed a French fry off his plate and shoved it into her mouth.

"Hey. No fair eating my food because you trashed your own."

"Partners share."

He reached across the table and covered her hand with his. "Some partners would like to share even more."

Kelly playfully poked his hand with her fork. "Not gonna happen, Romeo."

"You're killing me, Silverthorne." He leaned back in his chair. His sharp blue eyes focused on her face, much the same way they focused on a defendant he intended to break. "I've been asking you out for two years. When are you going to cut me some slack and let me take you on a date? I promise dinner, a movie, the whole shebang. I'll even be a gentleman even though it might kill me."

She laughed at the exaggerated whine in his tone. "Daniel. You are a really nice—"

"*No.*" Comically he covered his face with both hands. "Do *not* give me the *friends* speech."

His reaction sent her into a fit of laughter which helped to ease the tension churning the tuna salad sandwich in her stomach. Her phone chimed. She and Daniel looked at each other before she picked it up and checked the text message. "Jury's in."

One golden brow lifted. "Two hours to deliberate?"

Kelly nodded.

"Shit."

"Yeah." She tossed her napkin on the table and grabbed the check. "Let's go."

It took another two hours for the media to be notified and for everyone to reassemble in the courtroom. Kelly had stood outside in the warm June sunshine until the last possible moment. Praying. Searching for a lucky penny on the ground or a stray rabbit's foot. Heck, if it would mean a conviction she'd haul a whole danged bunny into the courtroom.

Her high heels clicked on the marble floor as she passed

through security, headed toward the elevator, and pressed the button. She reviewed the trial in her head while the floor numbers lit up like Christmas lights. With the exception of admitting two questionable exhibits into evidence, she'd done everything possible to nail Andrew Colson for the murder of his wife, Alicia. Over the past year Kelly had given meticulous consideration to the evidence. She'd role played. She'd spent hours and hours at the law library looking up comparable cases. She'd interviewed dozens of character witnesses. By the time she and Daniel had the case packaged and ready to present, she'd been confident they'd get a conviction.

Two hours to deliberate.

An icy chill shot up her back as the elevator doors slid open.

She wished she felt that confident now.

Inside the courtroom she set down her expandable briefcase and returned the anxious regard Daniel gave her when their gazes met. She sat down and busied herself with collecting her notes and her thoughts. Minutes later the defendant in his Armani suit and expensive haircut strolled in with his high-powered attorneys. He cast an arrogant glance toward the already seated jury then sat down and leaned back as though he were in a bar waiting for his scotch.

Geez, couldn't the guy even pretend to be human? After all, this was a trial for the murder of his wife. A woman he had pledged to honor and cherish all the days of their lives. His two children were now motherless and, if Kelly had done her job, they would be fatherless too. In a moment of sheer compassion, she felt bad about that. Not for the defendant, but for the children who would grow up forever wondering what had really happened to the woman who poured their cereal every day, taxied them to soccer practice, and tucked them into bed at night.

Kelly slid her gaze across the courtroom to where Alicia Colson's family sat together, holding hands like linked chains. They would be there for the kids. Thank God for that.

Judge Reginald Dawson entered and the courtroom stood until he was seated. Kelly gripped her pen in her hand and mentally began her customary chant.

He is guilty. He will pay. He is guilty. He will pay.

"Has the jury reached a verdict?" Judge Dawson's deep voice boomed through the packed room.

The jury foreman stood and sweat broke out on the back of Kelly's neck.

"Yes, Your Honor."

"Has the jury signed the appropriate verdict form? If so, please provide them to Deputy Southwick who will then present them to me."

As Judge Dawson opened the envelope and silently reviewed the documents, Kelly crossed her ankles and squeezed them together. Her heart pounded.

The judge passed the papers to the court clerk who then began to read. "We, the jury in the above titled action, find the defendant . . ."

CHAPTER TWO

Defendant not guilty.

They were only three words. But for Kelly they were three words that had taken all the wonderful things she believed about life and made them hideous.

Surrounded by the scent of caramel, and chocolate, and cinnamon raisin bread warm from the oven, Kelly propped her head up with one hand and shoveled another bite of chocolate chip cheesecake into her mouth with the other. When the golden retriever at her feet begged for a taste, Kelly guarded her plate like security at Fort Knox.

"Dream on, pooch."

The smooth dessert melted in her mouth while she studied the small office in which she'd sequestered herself a little over an hour ago. A calendar on the wall denoted "Sweet Sale" days at the Sugar Shack, the bakery established by her parents, now run by her kid sister, Kate. On the dinged-up desk sat a faded photo of her parent's wedding thirty-six years ago, and a photo of Kate's wedding to Deer Lick's new sheriff, taken just seven short months ago. Ceiling to floor shelves lined the back wall where a rainbow of sugar sprinkles, edible sparkles, and candy crunches lined up cap-to-cap next to an array of both PG and X-rated cake pans. Enormous differences existed between the Silverthorne women. While her mother had once created basic cakes with buttercream icing, her sister Kate's creations reflected her imaginative and often racy specialty cakes. Kelly, though she had a talent for making kickass fudge, couldn't fashion a buttercream rose to save her life.

She glanced back up to her parents' wedding photo and studied the faded print of her mother who'd died suddenly last fall. Mixed emotions rumbled around inside her heart as she thought of the last time she'd spoken to the woman who'd given her life. Well, the last time she'd heard her mother's voice. Kelly had placed her scheduled weekly call expecting their conversation would go as usual. Fluff calls, she'd come to name them because they'd become little more than generalities.

On that last call her mother had been too busy to talk. Several days later she'd returned the call but Kelly had been in court and unable to talk. It seemed like that had become the pattern of their relationship. Mom was always too busy, and when she'd find time Kelly would be unable to connect.

Kelly shoveled in another bite of cheesecake, closed her eyes, and swallowed her guilt. She'd worked in this bakery beside her family from the time she'd been old enough to hold a mixing spoon in her hand until the day she'd left for Northwestern University. Today, the place felt foreign and isolation echoed in her soul.

Her fault.

Like the inexorable loss of her mother, the events of the past month slammed through her head as if she still stood on that courtroom floor fighting for a justice that would be denied. Fighting for the rights of a woman whose life had been ripped away by a monster. A fiend now able to roam free because *she* hadn't convinced the jury of his crime.

Her fault.

She'd pushed for that arrest. Pushed for an indictment with the grand jury. Pushed for a homicide case without a corpse.

Nausea and half a mountainous slice of cheesecake roiled through her stomach as she visualized the disbelief on the faces of the victim's family when the verdict had come down. The family she'd promised that she'd get a conviction.

In her mind she could still hear the collective gasp echo across the chamber walls. She heard the grief and torment in the family's voices when they'd pointed their fingers at her and her fellow prosecutor and accused them of incompetence. Of failure.

She'd been so sure.

But she'd been wrong.

She'd never been wrong before. Never lost a case. Never led so many innocent people into such a clusterfuck of bad judgment, poor execution, and weak evidence. Not once since she'd been an intern with the state attorney's office had she ever been doubted. Until that verdict had come in. The eyes that followed her out of that courtroom and back down the hall to her office had been teeming with accusation and disappointment.

She'd failed each and every one of them.

Horribly.

She'd lost her touch. Lost her confidence. And she had no idea where to go from here.

Her sister's monstrous golden retriever pup curled around Kelly's feet and groaned as though he could read her thoughts.

"Nice try, Happy."

The pup looked up at her with big understanding brown eyes, but no one could imagine the agony and guilt that spun a toxic web around her heart. Not even the man who'd stood beside her in that courtroom for months. When the verdict came down, he'd shrugged as if it didn't matter. For him, maybe it hadn't. She'd been the one who'd had to face the family, the media, the critics. She'd been the lead on the case.

Her fault.

The office door opened and her sister with her shiny auburn hair and clashing pink apron barged into the office. The dog got up to greet her and his long furry tail swept the floor in a happy wag.

"When you said you needed to hide out, I didn't think you meant literally." Kate used her foot to scoot a chair out from the wall and she plopped down. She leaned her forearms on her knees and she studied Kelly for a good long moment. "You look like hell, big sister."

"I imagine that's an understatement." Kelly leaned back against the rickety chair in which her mother had sat to order flour and sugar for over three decades. "I haven't slept much since the verdict came in."

"You did your best, Kel."

"Did I?" The pressure between Kelly's eyes intensified.

"Yes," Kate insisted. "You used every bit of evidence you

had. Your arguments were clear and concise. You led the jury down a path where they could visualize the timeline and the crime. It's hard to win a murder case without a corpse." Kate leaned forward and wrapped her arms around Kelly's shoulders. "What more could you have done?"

"That's what I keep asking myself."

Kate gave her a squeeze then leaned back. "Well, you're home now. And if anybody in the press shows up to harass you I will personally kick their ass." Kate's brows lifted. "It wouldn't be the first time."

"It feels good to be home."

"You say that now, but wait until you're tucked into that lumpy twin bed tonight and you hear dad snoring from down the hall."

Kelly smiled for the first time in weeks. "Icing on the cake."

"Speaking of . . . I hate to impose but would you mind giving me a hand out front? I've got a few orders I need to box up and I still have to ice two dozen cupcakes for Mary Clancy's baby shower. Dad's busy with a batch of dinner rolls."

"You *don't* hate to impose, but I'd be happy to help anyway." Kelly shoveled the last bit of cheesecake into her mouth, stood, and grabbed an apron off the hook on the wall.

"Good thing you came home wearing jeans and a T-shirt instead of your usual lawyer regalia."

Kelly draped the apron over her head and nodded. She didn't think now was the right time to tell her sister she had doubts she'd ever wear another Brooks Brothers suit. Her colossal failure had led to a murderer's freedom—and there was no doubt in her mind that Andrew Colson had murdered his wife. She couldn't afford to screw up again.

Someone's life may depend on it.

She followed Kate out of the small office tying an apron around her waist and preparing herself to dive back into life in Deer Lick. She'd taken a leave of absence to attend her brother's wedding. But she'd also come home to hide. To lick her wounds. To overcome her guilt. If that was even possible. She hadn't quite planned to shovel cookies and cupcakes into white boxes, but that's exactly what she was about to do.

As she passed him in the kitchen she gave her dad a quick kiss on the cheek then headed toward the front counter. A glance over the top of the glass display case indicated a number of patrons reading the menu or pointing out sugary delights they intended to take home. Kelly's gaze skipped over the fresh Neapolitan ice cream colors of the shop, the vintage photo of her mom and dad on the Sugar Shack's opening day, and came to a sliding stop near the door. Back turned toward her, a wide set of khaki-clad shoulders blocked the summer's glare off the patrol car parked outside.

She sucked back a groan.

Apparently karma wasn't done playing *gotcha*.

Her hands stilled on the apron ties. Her heart knocked against her ribs. The knot in her stomach pulled tight. On the other side of the lunch counter stood another of her monumental screw-ups.

As if she'd called his name, he turned his sandy blonde head. His brown eyes brightened and a smile tipped the corners of lips that were sinfully delicious. She knew. She'd tasted them.

She took a wobbly step backward.

In her thirty-two years she'd been struck with accusatory

scowls from a judgmental mother and murderous glares from convicted felons, but nothing had ever hit her below the belt like a smile bursting with sexual promise from one of Deer Lick's finest.

Deputy James Harley.

His intense gaze perused her body like he was on the cruise of a lifetime and enjoying the trip. He'd looked at her that same way just a few months ago—braced above her on arms thick with muscle while the rest of his hot, hard body did the talking.

A tingle ignited from her head, sizzled like a fuse down the front of her shirt, and detonated beneath the zipper on her jeans. Her skin turned hot and a flush crept up her chest. All thanks to the memory of one night in James Harley's bed.

As a deputy sheriff he'd sworn to serve and protect. During the hours she'd spent rolling in his sheets, he'd done both. At least from what she remembered.

The night of Kate's wedding reception, Kelly knew she should have stayed focused on carrying out her maid-of-honor duties. But one too many glasses of exceptional champagne had dislodged a few of her bolts and screws and she'd completely given herself over to whim and mind-bending orgasms. Afterward, she'd made a promise to herself to get a serious handle on the sometimes uncontainable urges that never ceased to embarrass the hell out of her. Even if they did provide a real jolt of excitement.

She blinked away the sweaty memory of the hot, sexy man on the opposite side of the counter, sucked in a breath, and stepped up beside Kate. "What do you need me to do?"

"Could you box up that chocolate cake and then fill James's lunch order?"

Crap. "Sure." *Kill me now. Please.*

Her hands uncharacteristically trembled as she opened a pastry box and lifted Dr. Robinson's double chocolate birthday cake from the display case. She didn't know why her stomach was so keyed up. She'd spent the last seven years in the heat of the spotlight, prosecuting some of the dirtiest criminals in the state of Illinois, and she'd never once been nervous.

So why did taking a lunch order seem so damned intimidating?

With a smile she handed the pastry box over the counter to Dr. Robinson's nurse and rang up the bill on the register. She closed the cash drawer and wiped her hands down the front of her apron, leaving a streak of chocolate. When she looked up *hot cop* was standing at the lunch counter. Muscled arms expanded from beneath his short uniform sleeves while the fitted shirt hugged his wide chest and slim waist. Kelly knew that beneath all that khaki fabric was a talented body of pure strength and muscle. A *very* talented body.

God, her thoughts were a train wreck.

She grabbed the pencil and order pad. "Can I help you?"

A smile crinkled the corners of his brown eyes and a slow blink swept long, dark lashes across his cheeks. "You're back."

"Apparently."

He chuckled. "And you're not happy to see me."

"I'm not *not* happy to see you."

"Okay then. I'll take that for starters."

Oh, no. His days of taking from her were over. She was on a *save your soul and sanity* mission. No boys allowed. "And what would you like to eat?"

The spark in his eyes guaranteed she wouldn't need a Geiger counter to detect what he was thinking. "Sandwich, Deputy Harley. What kind would you like?"

"I'd like two tuna subs. No tomato. Two iced teas." He settled a lean hip against the counter. "And your phone number."

A laugh escaped before she could stop it. "That will be nine fifty-six."

"Is that a no?" He reached into his back pocket, withdrew a worn leather wallet, and handed her a twenty.

Her fingers curled around the money. "I'm sure you have all the numbers you can handle."

James held on to the cash, just to be able to touch her for half a second. "I'd be willing to throw all those numbers away in exchange."

Since she was a pro and could read a lie a mile away she probably thought he was bullshitting her. But he'd never been more serious.

One night with Kelly Silverthorne hadn't been nearly enough. Once she'd hightailed it out of town he'd tried to discount the hours he'd spent with her in his arms but it had been impossible. Now here she was again. And everything inside of him was buzzing with awareness.

As expected she looked up and studied his face like he'd been named a prime suspect. He knew that look. On the job he'd used it himself once or twice.

"Without all those phone numbers what would you do on a rainy day, Deputy?" Her head tilted just slightly and her ivory hair fanned like silk across her shoulder. "I'd hate to be the cause of your ultimate frustration."

"Nice jab, Counselor." James steadied his breath as he watched her delicate fingers punch the amount into the register and slide the cash into the drawer. Kelly Silverthorne was the most beautiful woman he'd ever laid eyes on. And he'd seen plenty. From the second grade he'd watched her, admired her, and had probably had a crush on her even though the only glances she'd ever returned had been rife with warnings to keep his distance.

The night she'd ended up in his bed? No one could have been more surprised. Oh, he wasn't about to complain. No way. The counselor was hot. And sweet. And way out of his league. Though he knew he'd had his one and only shot with her, he craved her like a decadent dessert or a fine wine. One taste was just not enough to satisfy.

He watched as she grabbed the sandwich rolls, cautiously sliced through them, and spread a thin layer of mayonnaise across the surface. She topped the bread with perfectly rounded scoops of tuna salad and carefully placed leaves of crunchy lettuce on top. Every movement was smooth and calculated as if she'd be judged on her placement and presentation.

In an attempt to gain control over his body and all the odd stirrings around his heart, he looked away. A quick glance at the two sisters revealed the vast differences. Kate, his best friend's new wife, was a bit taller and looked as if in a scrap she could hold her own. Her straight auburn hair displayed a meager reflection of her fiery personality. Whereas Kelly, a few inches shorter, teetered on the more delicate side. She looked like a woman a man would jump to protect. Her long ivory hair had a soft curl that made her glow like sunshine.

He smiled.

At least she'd lit up his world. For a night.

"So what made you leave the windy city and come all the way back to our little town?" he asked as she wrapped each sandwich in white paper as carefully as if she'd been swaddling a newborn.

"Just needed a break." She slid the packaged sandwich into a crisp white bag.

"Most people who need a break hit a tropical beach. Not some dusty back road to nowhere."

"Maybe *nowhere* is exactly where I want to be." She shoved the second sandwich into the bag a little less carefully.

Whoa. Was it his imagination or was he detecting some underlying aggression?

"Well, I'm sure your family will be happy to have you around for a little while," he said, watching her graceful fingers fold down the top of the bag.

She gave him no response as she set the bag on the counter, grabbed two paper cups, and began to fill them with iced tea.

"So . . . exactly how long of a little while will that be?" he asked.

The glass pitcher thunked on the counter and tea sloshed up the sides. "The length of my stay is really no concern of yours, Deputy Harley."

"True. But I'm more than willing to change that if you are."

A smile tilted her soft, full lips. "You really are incorrigible."

He mirrored her expression. "It's a cross I bear."

She set the cups of tea down in front of him and pushed plastic caps over the rims. "I hope you enjoy your lunch, Deputy Harley. Please do come again soon."

"Is that an invitation?" *Say yes, Angelface.*

Her delicate brows pulled together over sea green eyes. "Are you serious?"

"As a tortoise trying to cross the road."

"I'm sorry, Deputy—"

"I think we know each other well enough to be on a first name basis, don't you?" Her slight hesitation gave him hope.

"Like I said, I'm sorry, *Deputy*, I'm not here to engage in anything other than some rest and relaxation. I need a break. Not an opportunity to . . . lose control," she whispered.

James smiled. He knew exactly how loudly Kelly lost control. And exactly what made her lose it. Then again, he was more than willing to invent new techniques to make that happen too. Even if it took all night. *Please, God, let it take all night.*

If Princess Prosecutor imagined him as a man who gave up easily she'd be very wrong.

"You know . . ." He leaned closer and spoke low for her ears only. "If you give me your number you might just have a little fun losing a little control for the little while you're here." He lifted the bag and cups from the counter, stepped back, and gave her a good long appreciative once over. "Or is that what you're afraid of?"

An Excerpt from

A MOST NAKED SOLUTION
by *Anna Randol*

Lady Sophia Harding: beautiful, blonde, and . . . capable of murder? That's what Lord Camden Grey intends to find out.

Sophia knows that to keep her family's secrets she must avoid any entanglements with the powerful and brutally handsome man. But the pull of their mutual desire is all-consuming. Can Sophia trust Camden with the truth when she knows it might kill the love that grows between them?

CHAPTER ONE

Weltford, England, 1816

Sir Camden Grey glared at the ink-spotted paper in front of him. Damnation. Was that a six or an eight? Perhaps a three? He placed his quill back in the ink and pressed the heels of his hands against his bleary eyes.

He should have stopped working on the equation hours ago, but the solution had seemed so close this time. If he'd worked only a little harder or faster, perhaps he'd have been able to—

A knock again sounded on his door, reminding him of what had startled him into splashing ink everywhere in the first place.

"Yes?" He knew his tone was harsher than it should have been, but he hadn't slept in—he checked the clock—twenty hours, and his servants knew better than to disturb him. If that fool Ipswith found an answer first, Camden would never again be able to set foot in the Royal Mathematical Society. The chairman, his father, would see to it. Just as he had seen to convincing Ipswith to research the exact same theorem to put Camden in his place.

The door opened and Rafferty entered, his stoic butler façade remaining in place despite the crumpled papers littering the carpet at his feet. "There is a . . . man to see you, sir." There was a significant distaste in his pronunciation of the word *man*.

Camden raised his brow. What was he then, a goat? Really, it was no wonder he found conversing such a waste. It was an imprecise medium. "What is his business?"

"He wishes to speak to the Justice of the Peace."

Camden glanced at the clock. "At three in the morning? Has there been a death?"

Rafferty cleared his throat and didn't make eye contact. "It is three in the afternoon, sir."

Camden swiveled to stare at the drawn curtains behind him. Indeed. Amend that—he'd been awake for thirty-two hours instead of twenty. Suddenly exhaustion hit him like a blow to the side of his head. He scrubbed at the grit in his eyes. "Did he say if it was urgent?"

As impressive as the title of Justice of the Peace sounded, it usually only amounted to settling squabbles about sheep and stolen chamber pots. He wouldn't have accepted the appointment to the position at all if there had been any other men who met the requirements in Weltford save drunk-off-his-arse Stanfield.

"The fellow claims to have information on the Harding death, sir."

Camden straightened in his chair. That would be worth delaying sleep. "Where did you put him?"

"In the library, sir."

Camden stood, twisting side to side briefly to loosen the knots in his back, then strode past his butler and down the stairs.

He smelled his guest before he saw him. The air in the corridor stank of stale onions and spoiled ale. And he wasn't even in the same room yet.

Camden stepped into the library, then silently groaned when he saw his guest. "Mr. Spat?" Lloyd Spat, less than affectionately known about the village as Tubs, sat in the center of the room, his enormous girth filling the settee from arm to arm.

"Ah, Sir Camden! A pleasure to see to see you. A real pleasure." He tried to struggle to his feet but gave up after a single attempt. "There was a reward for information on the death of Lord Harding? A sizable one?"

"If your information proves to be of use." But he had offered the money over three months ago at the death of Viscount Harding. While he still found it difficult to believe the death was a result of a poacher's misplaced bullet, he found it more difficult to believe that Tubs wouldn't have come forward if he had real information. The man would do anything for his next pint. "Why wait to come forward?"

"Well, I feared for my life. Near trembled at the thought of what would happen to me if they found out I spoke."

"If who found out?" Camden focused on breathing through his mouth only.

"The men."

He was too tired for this. His only hope was a strict linear line of questioning. Camden spun the standing globe next to him absently, tapping every third line of longitude. He returned to the original question. "Why tell me now?"

"Well you might ask, sir. Mr. Haws, that greedy old bastard, has decided that my word is no longer good enough for him. He says if I'm wanting another drop of ale from his tavern, he needs to be seeing some of the coin he's owed. Now I'm rightly offended at such rudeness and I have a mind to take my business to another tavern, but my health's no longer what it was. And I need to be close to my lodgings and my dear Mrs. Spat."

So he'd decided that his next drink was worth more than information that might cost him his life. That logic would have been too much to follow on a day when fully awake; Camden stood no chance of sorting it out now.

Tubs rubbed his hands together, then glanced nervously about the room. "No one will find out the news came from me, right?"

"Not unless you tell them."

Tubs nodded, his chin disappearing into the rippling folds at his neck. "Well, then. The day after the murder I was at the tavern."

Camden had never seen him anywhere but at the tavern.

"I was sitting at my table in the corner when I heard voices behind me. It was two blokes discussing getting paid. Now I normally keep to my own business but one of the gents says, 'The deed is done?' Now I know that when men are talking about deeds, that's not something that I need to be hearing, but I was right there so I couldn't not hear them."

Camden stopped spinning the globe, his hand coming to rest somewhere in Russia. Tubs finally had his full attention.

It wasn't Camden's responsibility as Justice of the Peace to investigate crimes, only to rule on small squabbles, or for more serious matters, to decide if there was enough evidence for a criminal to be sent on to the formal court. While he gave the cases he heard his full attention, he'd never been tempted to become involved past his limited role. It was the responsibility of the victim or his family to prosecute the crime. But something about the Harding case had seemed suspicious. Camden had finally ruled with the coroner's jury because he'd had no evidence to contradict the theory of the poacher's bullet, but it had always seemed too convenient. As if someone had decided three plus three equaled five because they didn't want to be bothered to count to six.

Then the widow's powerful family had swooped in to ensure the whole matter stayed quiet. Her father and her brothers stayed at her side, keeping her distant from everyone. Lady Harding's father, the Earl of Riverton, himself, had visited Camden to ask for discretion when dealing with the case.

Camden had agreed because he knew better than to deny a powerful man like the earl without cause. He also knew the earl's oldest son, Darton, personally, and he trusted him.

To a point.

But the whole situation had made him wary. More alert. He'd asked a few questions about town but had come up empty.

Tubs cracked his knuckles, the popping interspersing his words. "Then the other fellow says, 'He fell like a sack of turnips. Easiest job I've ever done.' Then he laughed. Now I hadn't heard about the good viscount's death yet, but something in his voice made my skin fair crawl off my body."

"Did you get a good look at either of the men?"

Tubs's eyes bulged. "There's no way I was going to let them know I'd heard them. What with them being hired killers."

Camden could hear his own teeth grinding. "Then what information do you have that you think will earn you the reward?"

"Well, then they started talking about returning to London." He looked hopeful at this bit of information, then sighed when Camden didn't react. "Then one of the fellows said, 'Did you collect the rest of the blunt from her?'"

Camden stepped away from the globe. "Her?" Why had an image of Lady Harding suddenly appeared in his mind?

"That's what he said as clear as day."

"Did they give a name? Anything more specific?" Camden tried to think of what he knew of Lady Harding, but could come up with little. Oh, he could picture her clearly enough, the pretty young woman who'd lingered outside her brother's mathematics lessons when Camden had gone to tutor him almost seven years ago. The slender delicate grace of her body and the almost elfin point of her chin. He'd liked knowing that she hid in the corridor to hear his lessons.

But he knew nothing of the woman she'd become. The Hardings had been at their house in Weltford only rarely. He couldn't remember if he'd ever been invited to an event at Harding House. He'd paid little attention to the social engagements in the area. Besides, his knighthood was recent and that left him below the notice of the oldest of the blue-bloods like the Hardings.

And if he was completely honest with himself, he'd had

no desire to see the girl who'd written him the only letter he'd received while in the army—a love letter—with another man.

Tubs grunted and tugged on his ear. "No. They left right quick after that."

Camden had little reason to think Lady Harding the woman that the killers referred to. Except, why hadn't she or her family done more to find the shooter? Why had she been content with the coroner's ruling? Why had her family been so intent on keeping him away from her? They'd claimed her prostrate with grief. All his questions had gone through her father.

"Do I get the money?" Tubs asked.

"Only if your information proves to be correct." Despite his own suspicions, he had no proof that Tubs's story was true.

"But I took time away from my dear wife to come to help with your investigation."

Frowning, Camden tossed him a guinea. "For your trouble. But you get no more unless your information leads to an arrest."

The money disappeared into Tubs's pocket. "It will, sir. Everything I told you is as true as my name."

Tubs lumbered to his feet and Rafferty escorted him out.

Camden had planned to pay his respects to Lady Harding at some point, perhaps see what manner of woman she'd matured into. Now it appeared he had no choice.

She may have grown up to be a murderer.

"You want me to give away all of the books in the library?" Lady Sophia Harding's housekeeper stared at her in shock. "But, my lady, the books must be worth hundreds of pounds."

Eight hundred and sixty-three pounds, to be precise. Sophia knew. She'd purchased every one of them when they had renovated the house last year.

But now the gilded leather spines sickened her.

She took a deep breath. "Yes, every one of them."

"What will you put in here instead, my lady?" Mrs. Gilray asked.

Sophia smiled. She had absolutely no idea. She would pick what she liked. She didn't even know what that would be. Perhaps piles of penny dreadful or scandalous novels. More books on mathematics.

All she knew was that no one would have a say in it but her.

She wouldn't fret over her choices, thinking and rethinking each one. Trying to pick those Richard would approve of while knowing she'd never be able to guess correctly.

Richard was dead.

And now she intended to reclaim the library from his influence. Sophia traced a finger down the edge of one of the books. If only it was as easy to reclaim herself. "Send them to St. Wilfred's orphanage."

"Very good, my lady." Mrs. Gilray was too new to dare question her.

Sophia turned at the sound of heavy boots in the corridor. Her eyes widened at the sight of her head gardener.

Mud caked Wicken's boots and his white hair jutted out

from his head in awkward clumps. "There's an urgent matter I must discuss with you regarding the *rose gardens*."

Sophia tried to smile as if urgent meetings about greenery were a normal occurrence, but her mind was racing. "That will be all, Mrs. Gilray."

Mrs. Gilray's fascinated gaze swung back and forth between the other two occupants of the room, but she bobbed a curtsey and glided from the library.

Wicken closed the door behind her with a click, the kindly lines on his face deep with worry. "Sorry, my lady. I know this is most unusual. But I thought it important that you know."

Sophia swallowed against sudden unease. "Is something amiss?"

"My daughter just sent word from the village. The Justice of the Peace has been asking questions about your husband's death."

"What questions?"

He rubbed his right arm, the arm her husband had broken when Wicken refused to tell Richard where she was hiding.

Sophia fought not to stare, not to choke on the guilt that burned in her chest at the stiff way the arm hung at his side.

"What enemies Harding might have had. Same as he did right after the death."

"Has anyone said anything?"

"Not as far as I know, but it's only a matter of time before one of the villagers lets something slip."

Sophia's hands clenched into fists at her sides. Sir Camden wouldn't find anything. She wouldn't allow it. Not when that slip might lead him directly to her husband's killer—her father.

**Next month, don't miss these exciting
e-book romances only from Avon Books!**

THE WEDDING PLANNER
by Stephanie Laurens

Lady Margaret is proud to plan the town's most important nuptials—including that of a prince. But what happens when it's Lady Margaret who ultimately falls in love with the dashing Gaston Devilliers? *New York Times* bestselling author Stephanie Laurens once again wows readers with this well-crafted, steamy novella of finding love in unexpected places.

MATING SEASON:
A CABIN FEVER NOVELLA
by Alice Gaines

An Avon Red Novella

What should have been a productive research trip for Gayle Richards turns into something quite different when fellow professor Nolan Hersch tags along . . . eager to prove his theory that males are naturally more sexual than females. But when Nolan tests his theory on Gayle, he just might find that failure never felt so good . . .

NINE LIVES OF AN URBAN PANTHER
by Amanda Arista

Violet Jordan has had one heck of year: Discovering she's a shifter, her best friend is a fairy, and there's a whole other world out there she never could have imagined . . . not to mention falling in love. It's enough to make the former B-horror movie script writer question her sanity. But there's no time for doubts when the fate of her city—and the world—rests on her shoulders.

LAST VAMP STANDING
by Kristin Miller

Dante doesn't know what he is: though his fangs drop when hungry and he can go without sleep, he's not a vampire . . . not exactly. What Dante thirsts for is sex and violence, not blood. Stranded in a forest with Ariana, the jaw-droppingly beautiful woman he rescued, Dante is torn between two goals: discovering his mysterious origins and protecting the woman he is quickly falling for.